# Hockey Term at TREBIZON

# Hockey Term at TREBIZON

## ANNE DIGBY

EGMONT

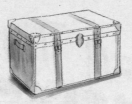

# EGMONT
*We bring stories to life*

*Hockey Term at Trebizon*
First published by Granada Publishing Ltd 1984
This edition published 2017
by Egmont UK Limited
The Yellow Building, 1 Nicholas Road, London W11 4AN

ISBN 978 1 4052 8071 6

www.egmont.co.uk

A CIP catalogue record for this title is available from the British Library

62831/1

Typeset in Goudy Old Style by Avon DataSet Ltd, Bidford on Avon, Warwickshire
Printed and bound in Great Britain by CPI Group

Stay safe online. Any website addresses listed in this book are correct
at the time of going to print. However, Egmont is not responsible
for content hosted by third parties.

Please be aware that online content can be subject to change and
websites can contain content that is unsuitable for children.
We advise that all children are supervised when using the internet.

MIX
Paper
FSC  FSC® C018306

# CONTENTS

*For Eva*

# **ONE**
## By Special Invitation

'Move over, Tish!' laughed Rebecca Mason as the four of them piled into the back of Miss Willis's car. 'And you, Sue! Give us some more room!'

She squirmed down into the little space between Tish Anderson and Sue Murdoch, her two great friends. With Laura Wilkins in the back as well, they were tightly packed.

It was all right for Jenny Brook-Hayes. They'd let her have the front passenger seat because her legs were so long.

Now all they had to do was to wait for Miss Willis.

'What a crush!' grinned Tish, lifting her arms up and placing her hands behind her black curly head, to make more elbow room for the others.

'So this is what they mean when they talk about

very close friends!' joked Sue.

'I hope we don't suffocate,' said Tish.

'Oh, who cares!' smiled Rebecca. She was bursting with excitement. 'It's not far!'

'I wonder if Joss will have changed at all since she's been living in the States,' murmured Tish. 'I wonder if she's got an American accent!'

'Not Joss,' said Jenny, from the front seat.

'I'm longing to see her again!' said Rebecca, with great feeling.

'We all are,' stated Laura.

Rebecca knew that to be true, and she knew the reason.

But none of them could possibly want to see Josselyn Vining as much as she did!

Ever since her sensational tennis victory, just after Christmas, Rebecca had been burning to meet up with Joss again. And now, quite unexpectedly, she was going to – it was fate!

'What's Miss Willis *doing*?' she asked. 'Why isn't she coming?'

'She's gone back indoors,' said Sue. 'I think the phone rang.'

Sara Willis was the head of the games staff at Trebizon school, very young-looking and energetic, with untidy fair hair. The car was parked directly outside her cottage in the school grounds. It was January. The hockey pitches and the school footpaths were deserted, silent and wintry-looking. On Sunday evening all the boarders would be back, ready for the start of the new term on Monday. But today was Saturday and the five girls in the car were the only ones back – they'd returned a day early by special invitation. That was why the school grounds looked so empty and peaceful.

But as they waited impatiently for Miss Willis to emerge, the noise inside the car mounted and made up for all the silence outside.

'He-llp! Rebeck, you're sitting on my hand!'

'It's Tish's fault. Move up a bit, Tish. I'm sitting on Sue's hand.'

'How *can* I? Laura's in the way!'

'And I'm squashed against the door,' giggled Laura. 'I feel like Flat Stanley!'

'You've all eaten too much in the Christmas holidays,' Jenny pronounced smugly from the front.

She yelled as Tish pushed her hard between the shoulder blades.

'We'll shove you out of the car for that. Then we can have your seat!'

'You can run along behind, Jen!' suggested Sue.

They all exploded with laughter.

Then –

'Sssh! Here comes Miss Willis!'

They sat up straight as pokers as the tracksuited figure came out of her front gate, clicked it shut, then walked over to the car. She ducked her head in – and looked slightly alarmed.

'What a tight squeeze. You've all got so big! Do you think we ought to take the minibus?'

A row of astonished looks greeted her, followed by a row of sweet smiles.

'Minibus, Miss Willis?'

'We're fine just as we are.'

'Deliciously comfortable.'

'Lovely car, Miss Willis.'

They couldn't bear the thought of having to unpack their weekend things from the boot! And then having to hang around while Miss Willis went and located the Trebizon minibus, which was probably locked up in the mews on the far side of main school, and which probably wouldn't start anyway. The idea didn't bear thinking about!

Sara Willis relented. She laughed.

'I hope my suspension can stand it,' she said, getting into the driving seat. 'Seat belt fastened, Jenny? Right. Let's go.'

The car shuddered over the track and joined one of the school roads. Rebecca had been holding her breath and now she let it out. She leaned forward.

'We're all dying to get there, Miss Willis.'

'I still think the car's rather full,' smiled the games teacher. They were travelling in low gear through an avenue of bare sycamore trees now, heading for the side gates which would take them out on to the Clifford Road. 'Happily it's not exactly a long journey. But if I'm doing the pick-up tomorrow, I think I'll bring the minibus. Just as well the whole squad couldn't come, that's all I can say!'

'Aren't we lucky to be getting this chance to see Joss!' said Laura, enthusiastically. 'There's so much to discuss about the sevens tournament at Easter. It's going to be such a help. I wonder how the Cats have got on today?'

'They're in the final,' said Miss Willis over her shoulder. 'That was Joss's father on the phone.'

'Fantastic!' said Laura.

'Won't it be great to see Joss again!' burst out Tish, as they turned out into the Clifford Road.

Miss Willis smiled once more and caught Rebecca's eye for a moment, in the driving mirror.

She guessed that Rebecca was the one who wanted to see Joss most of all.

Rebecca's parents were in Saudi Arabia. Most school holidays were spent with her grandmother, who lived in a small bungalow in a town in Gloucestershire. Living in the same town were some county tennis people who'd tended to take Rebecca under their wing in the school holidays.

It was thanks to them that she'd been able to enter the Midlands Under-16 Indoor, just after Christmas

– they'd arranged all the transport for her.

Up till then Rebecca had only played in Under-14 tournaments. She'd had a very good year and achieved some fine results. But having been fourteen in the summer, she would no longer be allowed to play in that age group from first January of the new year – it would have to be Under-16 tournaments from that date.

'So this will be good experience for you, Rebecca,' they said when they took her to play her first round on Boxing Day. 'It's an important tournament – E classification on the computer.'

Rebecca was excited and impressed. Up to now she'd only entered events that had a G or H classification and her LTA junior computer ranking wasn't nearly as high as she'd have liked it to be!

The last thing anybody expected was that Rebecca might actually win the tournament, which she did. It was a sensational victory. They brought Rebecca's grandmother over by car to watch the final and there were tears of emotion in Mrs Mason's eyes when she saw the trophy and cheque being presented to her granddaughter.

In the days that followed Rebecca had several phone calls (including one from her parents!), her photograph in the *Birmingham Post* – and a catalogue arrived full of beautiful tennis clothes, offering sponsorship and discounts. But it wasn't until she was telephoned by Mrs Ericson, her county coach in the west country, that Rebecca realised just how important her win had been.

Mrs Ericson wanted to check that Rebecca had sent her results sheet in to the LTA to get her new computer ranking. It had to be away by the third of January. Then she said:

'You were kept out of the Under-14 county side much too long. 'I'm sure you'll go straight into the Under-16 after this.'

'Will – will I really?' said Rebecca, in wonderment. The county was a very strong one.

'They may even give you some senior matches. You've worked very, very hard these past few months, Rebecca. I had a feeling that something like this might happen soon.'

It was her grandmother who brought up the subject of Joss Vining.

'What about that girl at your school, the one who went to America? You were heartbroken about that because she was so good and she helped you such a lot when you started. Well, when she comes back to Trebizon maybe you'll be able to beat her now!'

'Oh, Gran!' Rebecca laughed out loud.

'What's so funny about that, my girl?'

'Gran, you don't understand. Joss is brilliant. She was in the top sixty Under-18s when she was only thirteen – she's played in the junior hard courts event at Wimbledon – she's been to Eastbourne. And that all happened *before* she went to the States. Goodness knows what she's like now!'

'It doesn't seem fair that someone should be as good as that,' grumbled her grandmother.

Rebecca laughed again.

'She's brilliant at hockey, too. And athletics! No, Gran, it's not a bit fair.'

'Well, I don't expect she can be very nice then,' said Mrs Mason, brightening up a little. 'I expect she's got a big head.'

'Not at all, Gran! She's fine.'

Mrs Mason refused to give up.

'Well, at least you can try to beat her, Becky. It'll give you something to aim for.'

'I'd certainly love to play her again now,' said Rebecca, looking thoughtful. 'I've improved a lot. But how much? I can't know for sure until I play against Joss.'

'When will she be coming back to England for good?'

'Not yet, Gran. Early April, I think. She'll be back in time to play in the hockey tournament. You know – the one we've entered in the Easter holidays. The seven-a-sides. That's going to be fun! You'll be able to come and watch, it's only five miles from here.'

'I know.' Mrs Mason nodded and smiled. 'You've been chosen for that, haven't you? I'm looking forward to meeting some of your friends from boarding school. I've heard so much about them and I've never met them!'

'You will, Gran. At Easter.'

'And at Easter I'll ask Joss to give me a match,' thought Rebecca. 'I've got to know – I've got to! Oh, I wish it weren't so far away.'

So what a wonderful surprise it was when Miss Willis rang up with the sudden invitation!

It was during the last week of the holidays.

'You mean Joss is still in England?' Rebecca exclaimed in surprise.

The Vinings' home was in the west country, only about twenty miles from Trebizon. They lived on the outskirts of Clifford in a house that was formerly a small manor. Rebecca knew that they'd come over from the States to spend Christmas at home, but she'd taken it for granted that they would have flown back by now.

'They're staying on an extra week so that Joss can play in the Clifford seven-a-sides on Saturday. You know she plays for the Clifford Cats when she can? They'll fly back next Monday. I had dinner with them last night at Little Manor and when I mentioned some of the problems Laura had been having last term, getting our sevens squad together, Joss said why don't you all come down and spend the weekend at her place? You can have a pow-wow. You'll be able to see the Cats in action, too, and that's quite something. See how it's done.'

'Oh, Miss Willis, I'd love to! I'll have to ask Gran.'

'You're due back at Trebizon by Sunday in any case. It just means getting back a day earlier. Laura can come, she's delighted about it. So can Ishbel and Sue. I'm not sure about some of the others.'

So Tish and Sue would be going, too! Rebecca hastily conferred with her grandmother, telephoned the bus company to see if she could alter her booking, and then rang Miss Willis back.

'It's Rebecca Mason. I can be at Trebizon about

midday on Saturday.'

'Splendid. We're planning to leave after lunch. Jenny can come, too, so that's five of you. Rebecca, I quite forgot to congratulate you. Mrs Ericson phoned me last week. Wonderful!'

Rebecca reddened slightly. Then she said, in a tentative voice:

'Did you tell Joss?'

'Yes. Yes, I did.'

'Have the Vinings got a court by any chance?' Rebecca asked, rather abruptly.

'Oh, yes. A splendid one,' Miss Willis replied. She paused, then: 'You must ask Joss to give you a game. On Sunday perhaps. I'm sure she will. As long as the weather holds.'

'Then I'll ask her,' said Rebecca, trying not to sound too eager. 'It'd be interesting to play her again.'

'Very,' said Miss Willis.

'What a lovely house!' exclaimed Sue as the car swung in through the open wrought iron gates. There were stone pillars on either side of the gateway with moss-covered urns on top. It made a very grand entrance. Beyond, at the end of a narrow drive that ran between steep grassy banks, was a beautiful small white manor house surrounded by formal gardens.

'It looks quite old!' said Rebecca.

'We'll just dump your luggage at the house and then I'll drive you straight over to the sports ground and drop you all off,' said Miss Willis. 'The final starts at three and you don't want to miss any of it. I've got to get back to school and see to a few things, more's the pity.'

A maid came and opened the massive front door and asked the girls to leave their little bits of luggage in the cool darkness of the big hallway, Rebecca's tennis racket included.

'I'm just in the middle of sorting out your rooms,' she said with a friendly smile. 'You can see them when you come back at tea time.'

They came back outside into the daylight, where they had to descend a flight of shallow stone steps to return to the waiting car. Rebecca was last out and lingered for a moment at the top of the steps – gazing all around her eagerly.

The gardens looked lovely, with lots of trees and shrubs, and there was a terrace with a sundial in the middle. It must be beautiful here in the summer! Her eyes searched for something and then she saw a long golden beech hedge, with some dark green surround wire netting peeping up from behind it.

She glanced up at the January sky, bright behind a high cloud formation. The weather forecast for the weekend was quite good. No rain expected.

She descended the stone steps, very slowly.

'Come on, Rebecca,' Laura called out chidingly from the car, leaning out and holding the rear door open for her. 'Let's go and see Joss!'

'What were you looking at?' asked Jenny.

Rebecca jumped down the last two steps and hurried to the car.

'Nothing!' she said. 'Just – just the gardens.'

It was the tennis court she'd been looking at mainly.

# TWO
## A Disappointment...

'Joss – have you *shrunk*?' exclaimed Rebecca.

She remembered Joss as tall, towering over her!

'Of course I haven't shrunk!' smiled Joss. She took a step forward and put her shoulder against Rebecca's. 'You've just kept on growing, that's all. I stopped about a year ago. Thank goodness!'

So that was it. Of course, Joss was nearly a year older than Rebecca – one of the oldest in their year at Trebizon.

'When you two have quite finished, it *looks* as though they're waiting for someone!' said Tish with a grin, shading her eyes and training them across the sports ground to the farthest pitch, where the final was about to be played. 'Come on, Joss, let's get you over there. Someone's waving!'

They surrounded her and moved across the ground in a group, skirting round the abandoned pitches where the earlier rounds of the tournament had been played. They were now very churned up in places. The far pitch was lined with spectators. All the defeated teams from many different clubs were there, tracksuited in a striking array of club colours. They tended to stick together, colourful knots of women in purple and burgundy and light blue and bottle green, strung out along the touchline, acres of flat green grass all around them, meeting up with a great expanse of overarching winter sky.

A sevens tournament in the middle of winter was an exhausting business. A lot of play had to be crammed into the hours of daylight. Some of the teams had left home while it was still dark to get there for a nine o'clock start and had played several hard matches since. Mostly the tournaments took place in spring. But now this one had reached its climax. The final was due to start. It would be fun to watch someone else do the work for a change. They had that consolation.

The girls passed a harassed-looking father, dragging two small children back to the clubhouse. They were bored with watching their mother play hockey and beginning to get tired and irritable.

'I wanna drink of orange, Dad!'

'I wanna biscuit!'

They let them pass and pushed on. Rebecca had a good view of the pitch now. The Southern Universities Seven, the other finalists, with the initials SUS on their sweaters, were warming up – running up and down the field, flicking a hockey ball from stick to stick with casual expertise. They were female university students and they looked a very fit bunch.

The Clifford Cats, Joss's team, had gone into a huddle to discuss tactics. They were assorted sizes and ages. Joss was obviously the youngest member of the squad – if not the youngest person in the whole tournament. Their yellow and black strip was delightfully garish. Yellow socks with black turnovers, black hockey skirts and brilliant yellow tops with CLIFFORD CATS emblazoned across them in black. Some of them wore wide yellow headbands to match, as Joss did herself to keep her brown curly hair in place.

'I like your strip, Joss!' had been Tish's first words when they'd arrived, just as the Cats were filing out of the clubhouse to take the field. Joss had broken ranks and hurried over to see them. 'Who designed it?'

'My mother did. She used to play for them. She says she'll design some Trebizon strip for the Easter sevens.'

'We'll have to think of a good name!' Sue had exclaimed. 'Let's think of one – this weekend. How are you, Joss? You've grown your hair!'

'I'm feeling fine!'

'You're supposed to say "swell"!'

'Swell, then!'

They'd laughed and talked excitedly for a minute or two, and then Rebecca had commented on Joss's height and Tish had noticed that urgent signal from the pitch!

They were nearly there now.

'I'd better run!' Joss said. 'See you afterwards!'

'Good luck!'

'We'll watch and see how it's done!' Laura called. And they did.


'You're very quiet, girls,' said Joss's father as he drove them all back to the house in the big Peugeot.

'We're feeling most subdued, Mr Vining,' said Sue, sitting in the back row with Tish and Rebecca.

He chuckled.

'What did you think of the *Cats*, then?'

'Marvellous,' said Laura.

'Incredible,' said Jenny.

'Very educative,' said Tish drily.

Clifford had won 9-0. Now they realised why the Clifford Women's Hockey Club was considered one of the best in the whole country. And the seven players they'd fielded today, together with the two substitutes, must surely have been the cream of their talent!

'It helps having three West players and an England reserve in the team,' commented Joss. 'Anyway, one or two really strong sides didn't come today. They think we're crazy playing sevens at this time of year.'

Jenny Brook-Hayes was silent. She was puzzled about something.

'Why didn't the Cats have a goalkeeper?' she asked, suddenly. 'I mean a proper one.' Goalkeeper was her position in the Trebizon squad.

'Didn't need one,' said Joss. 'I'll explain later.'

'Let's talk it all through later. Let's talk and talk!' said Laura eagerly. She was Fourth Year Head of Games, captain of the squad for the seven-a-sides tournament at Easter and still slightly nervous about it all. It was a new national event for junior players and Miss Willis had entered Trebizon for it. 'This is the only chance we'll have, Joss. You must look at the team we've picked and tell us the best way we can train this term!'

'We can talk all night if you want to,' laughed Joss. 'But I'm not exactly an expert. Sevens is just for fun, really.'

All this time, Rebecca had kept silent. But now she said in a small voice:

'You've been keeping up your hockey in the

20

States, then?'

Joss had scored four of the nine goals in the final. Her play had been remarkable.

'Yes,' said Joss. 'Yes, I've been lucky.'

Mr Vining concentrated on negotiating the narrow lane that led to the gates of Little Manor. It was dusk now. An owl flitted right in front of them and Laura exclaimed over it.

'But really, you're mainly over there for tennis, aren't you, Joss?' stated Tish. 'That's what you're getting all the coaching for?'

'Yes,' said Joss. She was sitting next to her father and peering through the windscreen, ahead. 'Good. We're almost home.'

'Josselyn is playing with a big-headed racket now, you know,' said her father, informatively. 'It's a serious business. The hockey is just for fun.'

Rebecca's spirits dropped a little.

If the hockey's just for fun, she thought, what on earth can her tennis be like by now?

Both Tish and Sue noticed the chastened look on Rebecca's face and guessed exactly what she must be thinking.

As the car turned into the drive, Rebecca decided that if Joss did agree to give her a game of tennis this weekend, it would only be out of kindness. But she was still determined to ask her. She badly wanted to test her progress against the best junior player she'd ever played against.

So when Joss refused, it was a great disappointment.

Up to that moment of refusal, everything had been sheer pleasure for Rebecca.

They'd been shown to their rooms, high up in the house. She'd been asked to share with Sue and Jenny, with Tish and Laura in the room next door. They were quaint rooms, heavily beamed with tiny, high windows which – if you stood on the bed – gave a good view across the gardens of Little Manor. There was an antiquated wash-basin in each room, with old fashioned taps that said 'Hot' and 'Cold'. But with a great deal of gurgling and rumbling in the pipes they seemed to work and Rebecca was able to wash and comb her hair before they all trooped downstairs for a meal.

What a delicious meal it was, too! Round an old pine table in the huge farmhouse-type kitchen, the six of them tucked into venison pie with lots of vegetables followed by piles of strawberries from the deep freeze, grown in the kitchen garden the previous summer. The strawberries were served with lashings of creamy yoghurt.

Mrs Vining came in to say hello and then disappeared, and the maid took over after that – a new experience for Rebecca.

They asked Joss lots of questions about America and then they got down to the interesting matter of a name for the Trebizon sevens squad.

'How about Trebizon Trolls?' joked Tish.

There was a lot of giggling and argument.

'Trojans?' suggested Sue.

'Triumphs?' said Laura in all seriousness.

'That's tempting fate, isn't it!' exclaimed Tish.

'I know,' said Rebecca at last. 'Tigers!'

'Trebizon Tigers!' they all cried.

'That's a good name!'

And after a bit more discussion, that was the name that they settled on.

'What about strip?' asked Laura.

'Let's go and find my mother,' said Joss.

They crowded round Mrs Vining in the big drawing room as she went to work with a sketching pad on her knee and a handful of felt-tip pens, designing tops for them. They spent most of the evening on it! Finally, she came up with a beautiful looking top – dark green with white stripes down the sleeves and the team name *Trebizon Tigers* emblazoned on the front. It would go perfectly with the school's regulation dark blue hockey skirt and purple socks!

'D'you think Miss Willis will agree?' asked Rebecca eagerly.

'I'm sure she will,' said Mrs Vining. 'We discussed the question of new strip only last week. I'll show her this when she comes tomorrow. I'm sure she'll like the name, too! Brownings will make it up for you. It should be through by half-term.'

Rebecca felt very excited. What fun the sevens was going to be!

'When are we going to get down to business, Joss?' asked Laura anxiously. 'We're relying on you to give us some tips. It won't be enough just to look good!'

'Stop worrying, Laura,' said Tish. 'We're going to win!'

'We've got all day tomorrow,' said Joss. 'We'll go through stuff then.'

It was shortly after that that Rebecca's chance came. Mr Vining looked in and asked if any of them would like to see a video of some tennis, so she and Joss and Sue trooped through to a small television room. The three of them settled down to watch, on a sofa.

'What d'you think of Rebecca winning the Midlands Under-16, Joss?' asked Sue. 'You haven't even congratulated her yet!'

Joss rubbed her head with her knuckles, sheepishly. 'Neither I have!'

Then Rebecca burst out with the question that was so important to her:

'Will you give me a game tomorrow, Joss? Just a quick one? I've brought my racket.'

Joss looked at Rebecca doubtfully, then shook her head.

'I'd rather not,' she said, almost edgily.

'Oh, why not?' asked Rebecca, unable to hide her disappointment.

'But why?' said Joss. 'Let's give tennis a rest. We can have some games together in the summer term, if you like.'

It was quite final, the way she said it.

Sue raised her eyebrows.

Much later, at bedtime, she said to Rebecca:

'If you ask me it's not just her tennis racket that's

got a big head now.'

Rebecca, sitting on the bed and brushing her hair carefully, came to Joss's defence.

'Oh, it's not that, Sue. I think she was tired. Besides, she must be so *good* by now. You know what the standard's like in the States! I'm just not in that class, am I? I can't be!'

She said it wistfully.

Jenny was already in bed. From across the room, she stirred.

'Cheer up, Rebecca. We're all proud of you. Listen, why don't you write up that tournament you won for *The Trebizon Journal*? What it was like winning. All about it! You haven't written anything for *The T.J.* for ages.'

Jenny was Fourth Year representative for the school magazine.

'Would people like to read about it?' asked Rebecca, her interest aroused.

'Of course they would!' said Sue. 'That's a good idea, Jenny!'

Jenny didn't seem to want to talk after that.

She snuggled down in bed and pulled the duvet up over her head.

She had worries of her own.

# _THREE_
## . . . And a Few Words of Advice

'It looks a good squad, Laura!' exclaimed Joss the next day, glancing at the sheet. 'All those good runners.'

'Tish chose it, not me,' said Laura quickly, a tinge of colour creeping up her freckled face. 'And I didn't agree with it to start with, but I do now.'

'Past history,' said Tish, with brevity. She turned to Joss, who was always elected their Year's Head of Games without fail when at Trebizon. 'You think it'll do, then?'

The three of them were sitting around the kitchen table the next morning. Laura had produced a photocopy of the notice she'd put up at school at the end of the previous term. It was now lying on the table in front of Joss.

Joss studied the sheet of paper carefully and paused a few moments before replying.

It looked like this:

---

```
TREBIZON UNDER-15 TEAM FOR NATIONAL SEVEN-A-SIDES TOURNAMENT

    The tournament at Queensbury Collegiate, Gloucestershire,
    which was to have taken place on 17 December, has been
    postponed until 10 April which is the day after we break up
    for Easter. From experience this term I've found it necessary
      to make some changes in the squad. Here are the names,
                      with likely positions.

                          GOALKEEPER
                      Jenny Brook-Hayes

            RIGHT BACK                    LEFT BACK
            Aba Amori              Laura Wilkins (Capt)
                         CENTRE HALF
                       Ishbel Anderson


  RIGHT INNER/WING       CENTRE FORWARD       LEFT INNER/WING
   Susan Murdoch         Josselyn Vining      Eleanor Keating

SUBSTITUTES: Rebecca Mason; Wanda Gorski; Sheila Cummings

Full details of practices and training programme next term.
Please let your parents know the date and be free to travel
and stay overnight at Queensbury 9/10 April.

                                  Laura Wilkins
                                  Laura Wilkins
                                  4th YEAR HEAD OF GAMES
```

---

'Well?' said Laura.

Joss was silent.

'If you're thinking about Sue, she hasn't much music on this term,' said Tish. Sue was a Music Scholar at Trebizon. 'She'll get right back into hockey now! In fact she's hoping to get back into a school eleven.'

Joss *wasn't* thinking about Sue.

'Sue's a must!' she said. 'Lucky about the music.'

'Isn't it! Though we'd have played Rebecca in Sue's place,' explained Laura. 'But now Rebecca can be a sub. We want to keep her in the squad.'

'Oh, yes!' Joss agreed with that, too.

'So what are you frowning over?' inquired Tish with a smile.

'Mm, nothing.'

'*Come* on,' said Tish.

Meanwhile Rebecca, Sue and Jenny, who'd been out in the grounds, had just returned and were in the back porch. They were scraping the mud off their shoes on a metal scraper, just the other side of the kitchen door. The three girls inside were too engrossed to notice.

'Yes, *do* come on, Joss!' pleaded Laura.

'Well,' said Joss, 'I'm wondering about Jenny.'

'But Jenny's basic!' exclaimed Laura. 'Best goalkeeper I know.'

'Can't get much past Jenny,' commented Tish. 'She's good.'

At that moment Jenny marched in, followed by

Rebecca and Sue. Just as Joss was saying:

'In *goal* she's good. But . . .'

She broke off, disconcerted. There was a moment's hush.

'But what?' asked Jenny. She looked upset. 'But – ?'

'You don't always want your keeper in goal!' continued Joss resolutely. 'You're allowed to bring her out on to the field as a kicking full-back. We did that in the final yesterday.'

'I noticed!' said Jenny, as airily as she could. 'Remember?'

'You were going to tell us about it, Joss,' said Tish, with interest. 'It seemed to work.'

'Sometimes it's too risky. But you weigh up the opposition and if you think you can get away with it, you don't bother with a goalkeeper. You play her as a kicking full-back, which gives you the advantage of an extra player. Then you move your sweeper forward from full-back to centre half position – that's you, Tish. And then you go flat out on the attack! Try to make sure they never come in your circle!'

'And if they do?' asked Jenny drily.

'Well – you saw Beth Bingley yesterday. The times they got into our circle, she'd move back like lightning and was in goal to block off their shots –

that's not funny without pads, either!'

'She did all right,' commented Laura. 'Three good saves.'

'Well, we're just lucky,' said Joss. She was warming to her theme. 'She's really versatile, Beth! That's what you need for sevens. Someone who's just as happy out in the field as they are in goal.'

Jenny was silent.

'What are you trying to say, Joss?' Sue burst out indignantly. Her spectacles had slipped slightly and she pushed them up. 'We don't know anyone like Beth what's-her-name. We're just a bunch of schoolgirls! Jen's easily the best goalie we've got and that's good enough for me.'

There was a murmur of agreement from Rebecca. Jenny shot Sue a grateful look and sighed with relief.

Joss just smiled and nodded.

'Sure. Sure.' It was the first real hint of her months in America. It didn't go with Joss, somehow. 'Sure!' she said again. She pushed the sheet of paper back across the table to Laura and got to her feet. 'It's nothing to do with me, anyway. You're Head of Games, Laura. Thanks for letting us see.'

They all wandered upstairs then to get washed and tidied up for lunch. And as soon as Sue and

Rebecca had safely entered their room, Sue made a face and did a very good imitation of Joss.

'Sure!' she said. 'Sure – sure – sure!'

Rebecca laughed, but said: 'Oh, Sue, don't be unkind.'

'Well, really,' said Sue. 'What's got into her? *She* was being unkind. What was the point of talking to Jenny like that? It'll only undermine her confidence. Just because Joss is so good at everything herself!'

Rebecca's tennis racket was lying on the floor and Sue picked it up and looked at it meaningfully.

'That's the second time this weekend!' she said. She tossed it on to Rebecca's bed.

'Joss *hasn't* undermined my confidence,' said Rebecca stoutly. 'She didn't say anything to undermine my confidence!'

But Joss hadn't finished with Rebecca yet.

They ate Sunday lunch in the panelled dining room of Little Manor with Mr and Mrs Vining – a delicious traditional roast followed by apple pie and cream, and then chocolates were passed round.

'Our last English Sunday dinner for a while!' commented Joss's father. 'We'd better make the most of it.'

They were flying back to the States the next day.

'But we'll be back for good next time,' said Mrs Vining. She smiled, for she'd been missing her home a little and her garden most of all. 'It'll be the end of March and the daffodils will be coming out. And Josselyn will be back at Trebizon after Easter!'

'I'm looking forward to that!' said Joss.

Joss was at her best that afternoon, alive to the fact that their brief time together had almost run out. They spent the afternoon in animated discussion, sprawled on the carpet in front of a roaring log fire in the drawing room. Joss produced a pad and pencil, and drew diagram after diagram as they discussed team tactics and formations, surprise runs, the set piece at corners, how to score shock goals, how best to deploy the forwards, how best to deploy the backs. It was useful stuff, for none of them had played in a sevens tournament before, and it would give them a lot to think about and practise in the coming term.

They were mostly very fit, but they also made good resolutions to get themselves even fitter – early morning jogs across the sands at Trebizon, exercises in the gym. Rebecca smiled and mused that such a training programme, if they actually managed to carry it out, would surely do wonders for her stamina for competitive tennis as well.

Then Miss Willis arrived with the minibus at tea time, exclaimed in delight over the design for their new hockey strip, then collected them all up to drive them back to school. It had, all in all, been a marvellous weekend.

Rebecca stood on the top step outside the front door with her grip and tennis racket, taking a last look at the gardens in the dusk before descending to the waiting minibus. The others were already getting aboard. Joss was by her side, intending to wave them off.

It was then that Joss spoke to her.

Just as Rebecca was about to start walking down the steps, she caught her by the arm and restrained her.

'Rebecca!'

'Yes?' Rebecca turned round to face her on the top step. Joss looked very pretty, she thought. Still rather tanned from the months in California. Today in England there were cold little January gusts blowing her curly hair about.

The big porch lantern, which had once been a Victorian street lamp, was lit up. Sitting in the minibus, Tish glanced up towards the house and saw the two of them standing there, their faces caught in its illumination. She wondered what they were talking about.

'Look, sorry I didn't give you a game,' said Joss.

'That's all right,' said Rebecca.

'D'you mind if I give you a few words of advice?'

'Of course not,' said Rebecca. She felt suddenly uneasy.

'Look, there are other things in life besides tennis. Don't build your life round it!'

'But Joss, I'm a much better player than I used to be!' Rebecca protested. 'I know I was just rubbish before –'

Joss butted in.

'Don't fancy your chances in the States, Rebecca. Maybe you'd find you're still rubbish!'

Rebecca stared at her in surprise.

'Well, that's really telling me!'

'No! I mean –'

Joss banged herself lightly on the head with her knuckles.

'Rebecca, baby, I'm just trying to get something across to you. *Don't build all your hopes on something that maybe isn't going to happen.* I've seen a lot of girls play in the States and –'

Miss Willis sounded the horn of the minibus.

'Must go,' said Rebecca quickly. She felt a touch angry with Joss but she wasn't going to show it. 'Thanks for the advice, Joss!'

She turned her back on her and hurried down to the bus, suddenly after such a lovely weekend feeling deeply mystified.

'That's put me in my place, all right,' she thought. 'What has come over Joss?'

It was dark when they got back to Trebizon, strings of beaded light marking the footpaths that criss-crossed the grounds, groups of hurrying figures everywhere, brilliant squares of light picking out the sports centre as they passed it.

Miss Willis dropped them all off near the Hilary Camberwell Music School, a Spanish-style building that reflected its arches of light in the small lake that it fronted on to. Girls were making their way round it, going back to their boarding houses after tea.

'There's Elizabeth!' exclaimed Jenny, catching sight of the distant figure of her room mate walking slowly this way from the direction of main school. She rushed off to meet her.

Rebecca, Tish and Sue couldn't see any sign of their three great friends who shared rooms with them at Court House – Mara Leonodis, Margot Lawrence and Sally 'Elf' Elphinstone. They were probably still over in the dining hall.

'Let's go back to Court and wait for them there,' suggested Tish.

They skirted the music school and walked slowly along the narrow path that led through the shrubbery to Court House. Looming in front of them was the large figure of a girl. She was loitering along at a snail's pace so they dawdled along behind her, to save the bother of having to push past.

In any case, they were engrossed now as Rebecca told them what Joss had said. She hadn't been able to talk about it on the minibus.

'What a mean thing to say!' exclaimed Sue. 'There – I told you Joss was getting a big head.'

Tish frowned.

'Very odd. Not a bit like Joss. How can she possibly know what the future holds?'

'None of us knows what the future holds,' said Sue firmly. 'Rebecca might win Wimbledon one day.'

The figure in front of them stopped dead and they almost tripped over her.

She spun round.

'I do!' she said.

'Do what?' inquired Tish, with interest. The three of them peered at the girl. She was a total stranger to them. 'You do what?'

'I know what the future holds!'

'Rubbish!' laughed Sue. 'I don't believe you!'

They grouped round her on the lighted footpath, and when she was sure that she had their undivided attention she said:

'It's not rubbish at all. I can see into the future – well, sometimes I can. I've got the gift of second sight, you see!'

# _FOUR_
## Introductions – and a Present from Robbie

'Are you a mystic then?' asked Tish, putting on an expression of solemn interest.

The girl couldn't have looked less mystic-like. She was very large, especially in her billowing brand-new Trebizon cloak. She had a round, pleasant scrubbed-looking face framed by wisps of mouse-coloured hair – to look at she was very much the typically English schoolgirl, albeit an Amazonian version. She stood a head above them.

'We would never have guessed,' said Sue, starting to giggle. 'You look so Home Counties.'

'Of course I'm not a mystic,' the girl said placidly. 'But I _can_ see into the future sometimes. At my last school –'

'Hey!' interrupted Tish. 'You're not a Jehovah's Witness, are you?'

'They know when the world's going to end!' exclaimed Rebecca. 'Or at least they say they do.'

'Oh, *tell* us when the world's going to end,' begged Sue. 'I'd love to know. I wouldn't bother to do my prep the night before!'

They burst out laughing then and ran off, leaving her standing there.

They crashed out of the shrubbery on the far side, turned a corner, and then crunched across the sweep of gravel in front of Court House. Their boarding house was a blaze of lights and the front door was open. They could hear voices and laughter wafting across. Everybody was getting back!

'New girl, wasn't she?' commented Tish. 'Trying to make a big impression – trying to sound interesting!'

'Perhaps it's true!' laughed Rebecca. She was feeling cheerful again now, looking forward to seeing the others. 'Isn't she tall? Big impression all right! I wonder who's got *her*?'

'Well, it won't be us,' said Sue. 'She looks a Fifth Year at least.'

'She can tell them what's going to be in their GCSE papers,' said Tish.

At the front door they met Mrs Barrington, their House-Mistress, who was just about to close it in their faces.

'Oops, sorry. Come in, you three. Had a good time? I don't know *who* left this door open, but it's letting all the heat out! Doesn't anybody know how much oil costs?'

Somebody looked out of the Common Room door and into the hall and gave a joyful squeal.

'They're back!'

'Mara!' cried Rebecca in delight.

The three of them dropped their weekend bags under the stairs and surged into the Common Room, to be warmly hugged by Mara, Elf and Margot.

'About time!' said Mara.

'You missed tea!' exclaimed Elf.

'Don't worry, we've had some,' explained Rebecca.

'Mrs Barry says you've been spending the weekend with Joss Vining!' said Margot. 'What's going *on*?'

The six friends had the Common Room to themselves and sprawled around in armchairs and on the floor, talking non-stop and catching up with each other's news, while the colour television in the corner prattled and shone and flickered away all to itself.

While they were talking, Rebecca thought she

glimpsed three figures pass the window, through a gap in the curtains. It looked like Jenny and Elizabeth, who'd followed on behind them much more slowly, escorting the big girl between them. Was she lost or did she belong here?

And after a few minutes, Elf mentioned, 'By the way, there's a new girl.'

'She never said a word during tea,' commented Margot. 'She's so tall.'

'But I expect she will be an improvement on Ingrid,' added Mara.

Rebecca, Tish and Sue exchanged startled glances.

'You mean she's been put in Ingrid's room?' asked Tish. 'She's a Fourth Year?'

'I think we've met her!' said Sue.

'Oh dear,' said Rebecca, putting a hand to her mouth. 'We'd have been more friendly if we'd realised.'

They sprang up and went to look at the House List, which was on the noticeboard in the Common Room. 'Is her name Fiona?' asked Rebecca, running a finger down the list.

'Fiona Freeman, IV Alpha,' read out Tish. 'She's in our form then.'

'*And* on our floor!' confirmed Sue. 'In Ingrid's room.'

The room they referred to as Ingrid's room was, in fact, empty. It was the only single room on their floor upstairs, tucked away on its own at the end of the corridor and round the corner. It had been occupied by Mara for most of the previous term but then, for the last few days of term, by a Swedish girl called Ingrid Larsson who'd now left.

They returned to their seats and Rebecca said:

'We thought she must have been a Fifth Year at least.'

And even as she finished speaking the door opened and Jenny came in with her.

'Hallo, you lot,' said Jenny. 'Meet Fiona. I've just been introducing her to the other four upstairs. She's got the single room, isn't she lucky!'

Fiona was even taller than Jenny.

Dear Jenny, thought Rebecca. While they'd been lounging round and gossiping, their luggage still in the hall, she'd been up and unpacked, had a wash – and been looking after the new girl as well.

'This is Tish Anderson,' Jenny was saying. 'Her proper name's Ishbel. The three on the sofa, I expect you met at tea –'

'We've *all* met, actually,' said Sue, trying to look friendly and gracious in the slightly awkward circumstances. 'We met on the way back from the minibus. Hallo. My name's Sue Murdòch.'

'– the fair one's Rebecca Mason, she's our tennis star,' continued Jenny.

'Hallo, Fiona.'

'And now you've met "the six" you've met half the form. The other half lives in Norris House. You'll see them in the morning when Miss Maggs takes the register.'

'Who are all the other girls who live here?' asked Fiona.

'Thirds and Fifths,' said Elf.

'All the First and Second Years live in Juniper House,' explained Rebecca. 'That's a massive place at the back of the old school. After that, everyone's split up into houses like this one for the next three years – till the end of the Fifth.'

'The Lower and Upper Sixth have got their own boarding houses!' added Tish. 'They're allowed to cook their own meals and drive cars and go out a lot and have a pretty good time generally!'

Fiona nodded.

'We're all looking forward to that,' said Sue and laughed.

But it was hard work trying to draw Fiona into the conversation. She sat down beside Jenny and kept glancing at the television and tended to answer in monosyllables. So before long the six friends picked up the threads of their previous conversation, talking amongst other things about Rebecca's tennis.

Rebecca herself fell silent when this subject came up and Tish glanced at her and said:

'We'd better go up and unpack. And by the way, I've got something to give you.'

Sue stirred as well.

'I think I'll go and put my other jeans in the wash. They got covered in mud at Joss's.'

The three of them went out into the hall. Sue went through to the laundry room with her bag and Rebecca and Tish walked slowly upstairs with their own stuff.

'Not nearly so talkative when you meet her properly, is she?' said Tish. 'Fiona.'

'Well, we did squash her, didn't we?' replied Rebecca. She was wondering what it was that Tish wanted to give her. 'I suppose she just wanted to be included in our conversation – just said the first thing that came into her head!'

'Bit desperate, wasn't it?' grinned Tish. '*Second sight* – I ask you! I mean, how's one supposed to respond to that?'

'I expect she'll settle in and make friends all right,' said Rebecca.

'Not if she makes challenging statements like that,' replied Tish. 'Unless, of course, she really has got second sight. Now wouldn't *that* be interesting?'

'I suppose it would,' agreed Rebecca. 'Yes – very!'

Once upstairs, Tish kicked open the door of the big room that they shared with Sue and Mara.

Rebecca entered.

It was empty and peaceful, already in a pleasant state of disorder with Tish's half-unpacked trunk in the middle of the faded carpet. She could see into Margot and Elf's communication room and noticed that there were some brilliant new posters pinned up in there.

Rebecca flung her bag and tennis racket on her bed and gave a happy little sigh. It was good to be back! Then she sat on the bed and bounced up and down on the mattress a couple of times. At her window the curtains were undrawn and she knelt on the bed to gaze out, before pulling them across. It was quiet at the back here, a long stretch of shadowy garden below, the bare apple trees silhouetted in the faint light cast from Norris House beyond. Swish! She pulled the curtain across. That would keep the warmth in!

'You said you've got something to give me, Tish.'

'I'm just looking for it. It's in the bottom here somewhere.' Tish, was rummaging around in her trunk. 'I meant to give it to you before we went to Joss's, but there wasn't time. Ah, here it is!'

Rebecca got off the bed and went across. Tish handed her a small package.

'It's from Robbie,' she said, slightly embarrassed. Robbie was Tish's elder brother.

Then –

'He's missing you, the great worm. By the way, I've got a cake. Want some? I'll go and find a knife.'

She disappeared out of the room and Rebecca, left alone, sat down on the bed weakly and undid the string round the little package, then pulled off the wrapping paper. Her fingers were very slightly trembly.

It was a silver brooch. Tiny little tennis rackets, crossed. There was a card with it:

*Congratulations and love – Robbie.*

She stared at the card and held the brooch in the palm of her hand for a few moments, gazing at it. Then, hearing Tish's returning footsteps, she put both brooch and card in her bedside locker. 'It's a lovely brooch!' she said, turning away as Tish came back in. Carefully she closed the door of her locker. 'It's sweet.'

'Yes. He showed me. He rushed out and bought it after we heard you'd won.'

Rebecca had straightened up and turned round now and Tish saw that she looked rather moist around the eyes.

'He was stupid the way he went off with Ingrid that night,' said Tish. 'It spoiled everything, didn't it?'

'Yes,' said Rebecca.

Then, after a silence –

'But I asked for it, didn't I? I put everything into tennis last term and there wasn't room for Robbie or anything else.' She sighed. 'I suppose it was worth it?'

'Of course it was!' said Tish indignantly. 'Just *look* at the win you've had. You're really going places now –'

'Joss doesn't think so,' Rebecca cut in.

'Oh, stop thinking about Joss! She was just being mean –'

'But she's not usually mean, Tish. You know she isn't.'

'True.' Tish frowned, looking puzzled. Then she shrugged. 'Pessimistic, then. I don't know. That was just *her* opinion. You've got to forget it. Here – have some cake. I've got a knife.'

She produced an iced fruit cake from a tin that had been in the trunk.

Rebecca looked at it and shook her head. She didn't feel like any cake.

'Let's cut it later when the others come up. Let's have it at cocoa time.'

It was all very well Tish telling her to forget what Joss had said.

But it wasn't that easy.

# *FIVE*
## The Crystal Ball

Tish had just put the lid back on the cake tin when Sue burst into the room, laughing.

'Come on,' she said. 'We're wanted over at the sports centre. I'll have to unpack later –' She hurled her bag across the room towards her bed, over in the far corner. It bounced off the wall, knocked over her violin case which had been standing upended on the pillow, then slithered off the edge of the bed upside-down and disgorged its contents on to the floor.

'Blast!' she cried, and Rebecca and Tish laughed, scrambling over to help Sue pick up brush and comb, spectacle case, talcum powder and various other bits and pieces.

'There!' said Tish, stuffing things into Sue's

locker. 'You've unpacked after all! What's all this about, Sue?'

'What's happening?' asked Rebecca. 'Who wants us at the sports centre?'

'Laura!' said Sue. 'She's just phoned through from Tavistock. She's asked me if I'll round up the squad, and can we all be there in fifteen minutes. In tracksuits. We're going to have our first work-out.'

They changed quickly. Sue had already told Jenny and Aba, as well as the three Third Years downstairs who made up the rest of the seven-a-sides squad – Eleanor Keating, Sheila Cummings and Wanda Gorski. It was remarkable but true that apart from Laura herself (and Joss Vining) the whole squad was composed of Court House girls, which was going to be very convenient at times like this.

The three younger girls were ready and waiting in the hall when the five Fourth Years came down the stairs, Aba Amori bringing up the rear rather out of breath. She'd had trouble finding her tracksuit and even wondered if she could have taken it home to Nigeria for the holidays, but then Ann Ferguson had found it in the wrong drawer.

'Laura isn't losing much time!' Aba exclaimed, as the eight girls jogged off across the darkened grounds to the beckoning patches and slits of light that shone from Trebizon's large modern sports centre. 'I'm still stiff from sitting in aeroplanes and cars for the last twenty-four hours!'

'Then you need some physical jerks, Aba,' laughed Rebecca.

'We all do!' said Jenny, just behind them. 'We've been sitting round and eating all day, haven't we Beck? Not that Aba needs to worry.' The African girl was a superb athlete.

Wanda Gorski pretended to grumble.

'Laura's dead mean. You should have been made Head of Games, Tish! We're only just back. We'll collapse!'

But really the three Third Year girls were prouder than any of them to be in the squad for the national tournament at Easter and if there had to be a keep-fit routine then that was all part of the fun! They'd been very excited to hear about the new strip too and they liked the name *Trebizon Tigers*.

'If I'd been made Head of Games I'd have sent you for a ten-mile run along the beach to Dennizon Point and back by now!' exclaimed Tish. 'Not just a few physical jerks in a nice warm gym.' She could joke about it now. It didn't matter any more to Tish that she hadn't been made Head of Games, not now that Laura had agreed with all her ideas!

When they reached the gymnasium, Laura was talking to Miss Jacobs, the assistant PE teacher who ran the Trebizon Gym Club. Miss Jacobs was supervising Lucy Hubbard on the parallel bars and Rebecca noticed that Lucy, small and light-boned, was turning into a very good gymnast. She'd heard rumours that she was going to enter for some competitions.

There was always plenty going on at Trebizon - right from the moment everybody got back!

Soon the nine members of the squad were equally busy, working through a routine suggested by Miss Jacobs – a routine which began and ended with half a dozen exhausting press-ups.

'You can gradually build up the number as you go along, add one each day until you reach twenty,' she advised. 'And incidentally it's all rather more enjoyable if you have some music. Get one of your friends along to play the piano.'

'Ask Elf!' said Eleanor Keating afterwards. Sally was very popular with the Third Years in Court House, especially when she banged out pop songs on the old piano in the big Common Room on the ground floor. 'She can play all our favourites.'

'Elf would love every minute of it, wouldn't she?' grinned Tish. Then, in an aside to Rebecca: 'Thumping on the piano, faster and faster, and watching the sweat break out on our brows –'

'– and thanking heaven it's not her!' said Rebecca, finishing the sentence. They both laughed. Apart from swimming and surfing, Elf's interest in sports was minimal. Like Mara's.

'Verity's good, too,' Laura was saying. Verity Williams was a friend of hers in Tavistock House. 'She might like to come along. She's practising for her Grade six piano.'

'Press-ups and Prokofiev,' mused Sue. 'D'you think they'd go?'

'Why not!' said Tish. 'Anyway, we can get people to take it in turns. And if nobody wants to come, we could play some records instead!'

'I found it enjoyable enough anyway without music,' confessed Rebecca. 'I feel fitter already!' she declared.

She'd been missing some exercise all day. The food at Little Manor had been marvellous, but then she would have liked to work it off! If only she could have had that game of tennis with Joss . . . *Joss*. At the memory, she frowned.

'What's the matter?' asked Sue.

'Oh, nothing,' said Rebecca, with a shrug.

Soon after they got back to Court House, there was a phone call for her.

She hurried downstairs to take it, at the pay phone under the stairs. She wondered for a split second if it might be Robbie. Then she remembered that he'd said he wouldn't ring her. He'd wait until she wanted to phone *him* except that he hoped that it wouldn't be too long. That was what he'd written to her in a private note, at the end of the previous term. Well, she still couldn't bring herself to phone him. She'd thank him for the brooch, of course. She'd write him a letter. She'd have to think how to compose it.

'No, it won't be Robbie,' thought Rebecca, as she picked up the phone, which had been left off the hook.

'Rebecca?'

It was her county tennis coach, Mrs Ericson.

'Ah, good, I've caught you. Listen, Rebecca, I've heard that some people have got their new computer ranking. Have you got yours?'

'No, not yet, Mrs Ericson. I'm waiting for it.'

'You did send your results off by the third of January, I hope?'

'Yes!' Rebecca smiled. 'Definitely.'

'Good girl. Well listen, you'll be getting it any day now. When you hear, give me a ring. The best time to get me is in the evening, at home.'

'I'll ring, Mrs Ericson. I promise.'

Rebecca hurried upstairs, feeling slightly more positive about her tennis. She remembered that Mrs Ericson had hinted at some regular county matches, maybe even some senior matches. If that came off, she'd have a lot to thank Miss Darling for. Miss Darling, sometimes referred to by Tish as Miss Dreadful, was the tennis person on the games staff at Trebizon, a ramrod-backed, grey-haired lady. She'd given Rebecca special coaching all last term . . . and arranged for her to play against good adults, as well, at weekends.

Of course, that was why she'd seen so little of Robbie.

But she'd won the Midlands Under-16s, hadn't she? She'd *won* it!

'Rebecca, Tish is going to cut her cake!' cried Elf, looking out of their little Common Room on the first floor. Elf was in her pyjamas and dressing gown. 'Get ready for bed and then you can have some. Margot's brewing up a huge saucepan of cocoa – enough for the whole floor – we're going to have a feast!'

Rebecca collected her night things and then dived into the bathroom and took a quick shower and washed her hair before getting into her pyjamas. Now she felt good!

When she went along the landing to the Common Room it was packed tight with girls – all the Fourth Years in Court House, by the look of it.

Jenny and Elizabeth, the three As, and her 'six' as well. Margot was passing round cups of cocoa and Tish was passing round fat slabs of iced fruit cake. She'd cut it into twelve. Crumbs were dropping everywhere and cocoa being splashed in the general crush.

'Careful, Jenny!' cried Margot. 'You've made me spill some on my new dressing gown!'

'Hurry up, Rebeck,' beamed Tish. 'We were just about to eat your cake. Here –' she thrust it at her and Rebecca took it eagerly. 'Now, just one piece left. Who's missing –?'

'Fiona!' said Mara, with a start. 'Fiona's missing. Nobody has told her! You see? I think it is *horrible* being in that single room on your own. I shall go and fetch her –'

She was wedged down on the floor between two chairs and tried to struggle to her feet, cocoa in one hand and cake in the other. 'Help. Can somebody take these, please?'

'It's all right, Mara!' said Rebecca, who was right by the door. 'I'll go!'

'*Thank* you, Rebecca,' said Mara, looking at her with those lovely soft brown eyes. 'I am grateful!' She subsided again.

Laughing, Rebecca hurried along the corridor and turned the corner at the end, still clutching her cake. She knocked on Fiona's door and then looked in.

'Come on!' she exclaimed. The large new girl was in her dressing gown, boiling the kettle in there, tea bag at the ready. 'You can switch that off! We've made you some cocoa – there's some cake, as well. We're having a feast. We nearly forgot you! Isn't this a nice room?'

'Yes,' nodded Fiona. 'I like it.'

She turned the kettle off and looked pleased.

'I've got a big bag of crisps, shall I bring those?'

'Yes, please!'

It wasn't at all bad in the single room, reflected Rebecca as they walked back along the corridor together. Plenty of privacy – your own room! Some years the girls fought over it, according to Mrs Barry. It was just that they were a very gregarious crowd this year and preferred to share with friends. But she was glad that the new girl seemed happy in there.

'Crisps!' cried Elf in delight, as they squashed in to join the others.

There was a lot of chatter and laughter for the next few minutes, although Fiona didn't really say much, preferring to survey them all impassively. But in fact after the three As and Jenny and Elizabeth had drifted off to their rooms, she was still there and so presumably – thought Rebecca – must be enjoying herself in a quiet way.

Then suddenly she said:

'Did you know I can tell fortunes? Shall I tell somebody's fortune?'

Tish and Sue exchanged uneasy glances. Not that business of second sight again surely! But Mara squealed and clapped her hands in delight.

'Oh yes, Fiona. Tell somebody's fortune! Whose fortune will you tell?'

Fiona turned and walked across to Rebecca, who was now sitting in an armchair, and knelt down in front of her.

'I'll tell yours, Rebecca. Give me your hand.'

Rebecca smiled and held out her right hand, palm upwards. Fiona took hold of it and bowed her head, examining the lines on Rebecca's palm with intense concentration.

'I need something that would do for a crystal ball,' she said solemnly.

'I know!' cried Mara. 'A glass ball, yes? I know just the thing. It's in the bathroom!'

She rushed out and came back a few moments later with a clouded glass globe. It was the old bathroom light fitting, the cracked one, which had been on top of the cupboard there for some time.

It did look surprisingly like a fortune-teller's crystal ball.

# SIX
## Something More Important

'The very thing,' said Fiona. She stood up and she looked a commanding figure. 'Could you put it on the little table, please?'

Mara complied, setting the globe on the table, so that it stood securely on its neck, upside down. Fiona came and knelt down behind it.

'Can you come and kneel opposite me, Rebecca?' she said. 'Do you mind?'

Rebecca obeyed.

Fiona was now staring into the misted glass with such intense concentration that everybody became very quiet. She seemed to be taking it all so seriously!

'Now, Rebecca, just place your palm lightly on the side of the glass,' she said. As Elf and Margot started whispering to each other, she added: 'D'you mind being quiet, please? I have to have complete silence. Otherwise my powers won't work.'

They were all quiet again, as Fiona frowned and frowned. Rebecca kept very still, holding her breath.

Mara bit her lip nervously. She was beginning to find this slightly creepy. Fortune-telling was supposed to be fun!

Suddenly Fiona spoke excitedly.

'Now I can see it! It's something that affects your future, Rebecca. It's a piece of paper – and it has a number on it –'

Rebecca gasped.

'My computer ranking!' she exclaimed.

'Fantastic!' cried Elf. 'Honestly, Fiona, that's brilliant.'

They were all craning their necks now, trying to see into the globe, even Tish and Sue. This was fascinating. How could the new girl have known that Rebecca was due to get her new British junior computer ranking this month? A piece of paper with a number on it!

'What's the number?' asked Rebecca in delight. 'Can you see it? What is it?'

Mara drew back, eyes wide and a touch of fear in them, but nobody noticed.

'The number's rather misty –' said Fiona. 'I shall have to concentrate very hard –'

They waited eagerly. Mara was frowning to herself now.

'Can you see it yet?' prompted Rebecca.

'It's very tiny – yes, it's that computer writing – it's still out of focus. We have to be patient . . .'

The seconds ticked by. The tension began to mount.

Then suddenly, somebody burst out laughing.

Mara!

'*You cheat!*' she cried. Her eyes were shining with relief now. 'You nearly had us fooled. You can't see anything in that crystal ball –'

'Sssh!' said Fiona. 'You'll ruin the atmosphere –'

But Mara was giggling uncontrollably.

'Elf! Elf! Back me up. We were talking about Rebecca, don't you remember? In the downstairs Common Room!'

'That's right!' Elf recalled. 'We were wondering what Rebecca's new ranking would be!'

Mara pointed her forefinger at Fiona.

'And *she* was sitting with her back to us, watching the TV. She heard. *That's* how she knows!'

'Oh!' said Elf, disappointed. 'So that's how?'

'Oh, come on!' laughed Tish. 'Here, have a crisp.' They all started talking and laughing at once as Tish danced around the room, distributing the last of the crisps.

All the tension had gone. The atmosphere *was* ruined! Fiona looked quite glum.

'I want to know the number!' wailed Rebecca. 'Can't you lot shut up?'

But at that moment Mrs Barry appeared and shooed them all out of the room.

'Come on, bedtime! You've got lessons in the

morning! I'll wash those cups up, just this once.'

So the little party broke up.

But before they split up on the landing, Fiona whispered to Rebecca:

'I'll keep this in my room. Perhaps we can have another session. We'll keep on trying!'

She was clutching the cracked bathroom globe.

Rebecca stared at it in surprise, then smiled.

'Thanks, Fiona,' she said.

In their room that night Mara fell asleep almost immediately but Rebecca, Tish and Sue talked for a while in the darkness. Before she went to sleep Tish said:

'I think I was a bit hard on Fiona Freeman. She really seems quite serious about this fortune-telling business – and it's quite interesting, isn't it? I mean, I wonder if she *did* overhear Mara and Elf talking or whether she's got ESP – you know, extra sensory perception. Some people have!'

Tish loved it when unexpected or exciting things happened, and she added: 'It's going to liven the place up a bit if she has, isn't it?'

Rebecca yawned.

'I'd still like to know what my new computer ranking's going to be!'

'Well, perhaps it'll be in tomorrow's post.' said Sue, with admirable common sense.

It wasn't.

In fact Rebecca got tired of scanning the Court House mail board every morning to see if the buff-coloured envelope had arrived for her. Perhaps the computer hadn't got to the Under-16s yet.

And there were so many other things to occupy her mind, as she plunged back into her GCSE régime. There were more coursework assignments this term. The marks counted towards your final results next year. It didn't let you relax! So although it was exciting when Miss Welbeck announced in Assembly on the Monday morning that Rebecca had won that tennis tournament, she hadn't done her holiday work and she was falling behind with her French verbs. Rebecca that is – not Miss Welbeck. Her maths wasn't too hot, either. Then she made some really stupid errors on a Latin translation for Mr Pargiter, which upset him, and Rebecca realised that she must spend some evenings in the library – her favourite place for a quiet study – away from the distractions of Court House. She really liked Mr Pargiter.

'You should see how hard Robbie is working,' Tish said, to cheer her up. 'He worked all the holidays – he even gave up his job on the farm! He's got to do really well in the exams at Garth this term.'

'Why's that?' asked Rebecca. She was thinking 'It's just as well I've no intention of ringing him up then.' 'Why's he got to do well?'

'He wants to go to Oxford or Cambridge when he leaves the Upper Sixth.'

'But he's only halfway through the Lower Sixth.'

'Yes, but Dr Simpson decides at the end of this term which boys should try for Oxbridge and they go in a special group.'

'Oh, does that happen here?' asked Rebecca.

'I think so,' said Tish.

'I'm going to write to him soon,' said Rebecca.

On top of school work there were hockey practices, keep-fit sessions (nobody wanted to play the piano after all!) and some tennis coaching with Miss Darling as well. She was very pleased with Rebecca's result in the holidays and rewarded her with a rare smile.

One way and another, Rebecca saw very little of Fiona Freeman outside of the form room during the first week, but Sue told her that she was proving very popular with the juniors.

'She's telling all their fortunes! She spends half her time over at Juniper.'

'She's not dragging the crystal ball round with her?' asked Rebecca.

'No! She keeps that in her room. She's reading their palms, I think.'

'Sweet,' said Rebecca. Then she frowned. 'But why's she spending so much time with the juniors? She's not getting left out, is she? I hope Elizabeth's invited her to her party!'

It was Elizabeth Kendall's birthday on Friday.

'The juniors just seem to like her,' said Sue. 'They've already booked her up for their Charity Week next term! But don't worry – Elizabeth's booked her up, too. For her party. She's going to bring the crystal ball and dress up as a proper fortune-teller!'

'That'll be fun,' said Rebecca enthusiastically. She laughed. 'Perhaps Fiona will be able to tell me when this horrible weather's going to end, never mind the world!'

'Perhaps she will,' said Sue. 'If you really want to know!'

But Fiona was going to be able to tell Rebecca something much more important than that.

# SEVEN
## Tish is Impressed

It was early on Friday morning and Fiona Freeman was lying awake in bed, thinking.

Her curtains were only half drawn and she watched the day break, grey and leaden. She'd been lying awake for some time, listening to the rain in the quietness – heavy, splashing drops that splattered and plopped on the windowsill, on and on relentlessly.

She was feeling a little homesick. The Bluebells would be playing tomorrow, without her! She was going to miss those Saturday games. Her father's sudden posting abroad and her being sent to boarding school had put a stop to them.

Well, she wouldn't be playing her favourite game here, that was certain! She'd put her name down for netball, but it would be rather tame after playing for the Bluebells. Hockey didn't appeal to her. She'd try and steer clear of that.

She hoped she'd make some friends soon.

The crowd on her dinner table didn't take much notice of her. The Nathan twins were all right. The trouble was they were all in a different house – Norris, wasn't it?

She wished she could have been put on Tish Anderson's table. She'd liked this crowd in Court House right at first sight. But they all seemed so good at things!

At least her being able to tell fortunes had made an impression. People loved it. It amazed them.

It hadn't gone down too well with Mara, though. Never mind.

Tonight she'd be going to Elizabeth Kendall's birthday party on the strength of it! She'd never have had an invitation otherwise, would she?

She would astound them all!

'Mara! We're getting our party clothes filthy, crawling round this floor!' protested Tish. 'And we're supposed to go now!'

'My butterfly hair slide!' moaned Mara. 'I must

find it. Curly bought it for me!'

'Oh, Mara! You're impossible!' laughed Sue, getting up and dusting herself down.

Rebecca just smiled to herself, taking a last look under Mara's bed to see if the slide could be there. Trust Mara to have the four of them turning the room upside-down looking for it, when they should be on their way to the party by now!

Suddenly the door burst open and Margot and Elf appeared, calling out excitedly and dragging in Fiona.

'Well, what do you think?' asked Margot. 'Does she look good or does she look good?'

'Fiona!' exclaimed Rebecca, clapping her hands in delight.

They surrounded the big girl. Her appearance was now completely transformed in dressing-up clothes borrowed from the Drama Club. She was wearing some make-up, too, and looked really mysterious and exotic, especially holding the huge crystal ball. Only Mara ignored her, peering disconsolately into her bedside locker now.

'Look, Mara,' said Rebecca. 'Doesn't Fiona look good!'

She brought Fiona over and Mara straightened

up and turned round – and nearly jumped out of her skin. Mara was quite small and this evening Fiona was wearing high-heeled shoes to complete her costume. She towered over her like an apparition!

'I – I didn't recognise you!' she apologised, when she'd recovered; then said scoldingly: 'If you really have second sight, Fiona, you will look in that crystal ball of yours and tell me where to find my hair slide.'

'What does it look like?' asked Fiona solemnly.

'It's got a bright red butterfly on it,' said Tish. 'They sell them in Woolworth's – it's got great sentimental value.'

'Oh, leave it,' said Mara quickly. 'Come on, let us get to the party.'

They wended their way across the dark grounds, by way of the lamplit footpaths, to Moffatt's – the big school cafeteria and shop – where the party was to be held.

'Cheer up, Mara,' said Rebecca, as they walked along. 'You look marvellous anyway in your new dress – doesn't red suit you! Curly's never going to notice that you're not wearing the slide.'

'But he bought it for me. He loves me to wear it!'

Some of the Fourth Year boys at Garth College

had been invited to Elizabeth's birthday party – including Curly Watson. He and Mara were devoted to each other. Mr Leonodis was a very rich Greek shipowner and Rebecca knew that Mara had lots of valuable jewellery back home in Athens. But the cheap butterfly hair slide – bought by Curly with the last of his pocket money one month, simply because Mara had fallen in love with it – meant more to her than jewels!

'Are you sure you brought it back to school this term?'

'Of course I did,' said Mara. 'I've been wearing it in the evenings all this week.'

'That's right!' remembered Rebecca. 'Oh, it must have dropped off around school somewhere. Don't *worry*, Mara. I expect it'll turn up in Lost Property!'

Then Mara gave a little squeal of happiness.

'Look, Rebecca! Here come the boys. Mr Slade has brought them over!'

A minibus was just drawing up outside Moffatt's, crammed full of boys and driven by the House Master of Syon House at Garth College. They all fell out noisily, some of them with guitars. It was going to be a good party, thought Rebecca. The girls arrived at about the same time and there was loud clapping, cheering and whistling from the boys at the sight of the statuesque Fiona in her magnificent outfit. They all jostled into Moffatt's together.

'We're going to have some fortune-telling then?'

'Happy birthday, Liz!'

'What have you done with Moffatt's?'

The school shop was transformed. It was decorated with streamers and lanterns that cast a soft glow, lighting up the long trestle table, groaning with food, which had a huge iced birthday cake as its centrepiece.

It was a lovely party – lots to eat and drink, plenty to talk about, good records to be played. Rebecca enjoyed seeing Mike Brown, Chris Earl-Smith and Curly Watson again – they were great friends of 'the six'. The boys got their musical act together at one point and everyone stood and listened and tapped their feet.

Fiona's fortune-telling went down well, too. She set up her crystal ball on the shop counter, was kept well supplied with food – and had a steady trickle of visitors throughout the evening.

'She knew I'd been playing rugby this afternoon!' said Mike Brown, admiringly.

'Well, that's easy, Mike,' laughed Sue. 'You've still

got the mud under your fingernails, you disgusting boy.'

At the end of the evening, when the party had petered out, just leaving a few of them drinking coffee and listening to records, Fiona peered deeply into her crystal ball and said to Sue:

'You've lost the rosin for your violin.'

'How did you know that?' exclaimed Sue. Then: 'All right then. But tell me where it is.'

The room had grown quiet and people gathered round as Fiona concentrated hard.

'I think I can see it. Yes – it's slipped down behind a radiator. I can't tell you where the radiator is, but it's definitely behind one.'

'What about the radiator in our room, Sue?' said Tish, fascinated. 'Let's look when we get back!'

Fiona had got their undivided attention now. And as Sue took her hand off the crystal ball and moved away, Fiona called out excitedly:

'Rebecca! I must have Rebecca.'

Rebecca walked up to the counter.

'That's it. Now touch the glass with your fingertips. Hmm . . . I can see a sheet with names and numbers on it. I can see your name, and it's got your number beside it.'

'My computer ranking again!' giggled Rebecca.

'Ssh!' said Fiona, very seriously.

All went quiet now in the dimly lit room. The atmosphere was suddenly a bit eerie.

'Well, can you see what the number is?' said Rebecca. Her throat felt dry. Oh, this was ridiculous! It was just a game, wasn't it? But her heart was beating hard. 'You couldn't last time!'

'*Mason, Rebecca*,' said Fiona, looking deep into the glass.

'It's swimming into focus – now I can see it –' She groaned with concentration. 'Uh . . .'

Everybody held their breath. Curly had his arm round Mara's shoulders and he felt her slender body go rigid.

'Sixty-five!' gasped Fiona, in triumph.

There was a moment's stunned silence and then Rebecca let out an explosive snort. And on the faces all around her the tension evaporated.

'*Fiona Freeman!*' she laughed. 'You'd got me all excited. Sixty-five my eye!'

'But that's the number –'

'Not a hope!' retorted Rebecca. 'I've never been in the top hundred – and I'm an age group up now. I can't be number sixty-five in my age group in the whole of Britain – no way.'

Mara started to giggle.

'But it *is* sixty-five,' said Fiona, looking down again into the glass, '– and wait a minute, there's another number. I can see *two* numbers!'

'What a bit of luck!' Mara whispered mischievously to Curly. 'Now she can change her mind!'

'Sssh, Mara!' said Tish. 'How d'you mean, two numbers, Fiona? Rebecca can only be given one computer ranking can't she – not two!'

'But she's got two numbers!' said Fiona stubbornly. 'The first is sixty-five – and now I can see another number –'

All around people started talking and laughing, losing interest. Even Rebecca.

'A hundred and twenty-six!' said Fiona. 'A *hundred and twenty-six Mason, Rebecca.*'

'That's more like it!' teased Rebecca.

'Make up your mind, Fiona!' chuckled Elizabeth. 'Or we'll begin to doubt your powers.'

But she'd had a marvellous birthday party. It had all been a great success.

There was more rain on Saturday but it didn't affect Rebecca. She went by train to Exonford for a county tennis tournament on the covered courts. Mrs Ericson was there.

'You should have had your new ranking by now, Rebecca,' she said. 'Are you quite sure you remembered to send a stamped addressed envelope?'

'Quite sure!' said Rebecca. 'A big one – nine by four – like you're told to.'

'Well if it doesn't arrive in Monday's post, you'd better ring me up and I'll have to ring the LTA in London and chase it up.'

On Sunday morning the skies cleared and a wintry sun came out – the heavy metallic sea sparkled as the sevens squad went for a training run along the sands after breakfast. The wind whipped up the waves into a heaving silvery froth, and whipped the girls' cheeks and made them glow and sting. It was exhilarating!

'This wind and sun should soon dry the pitches out!' exclaimed Laura. 'They might be playable by this afternoon. Trisha says she'll get a team together if they are!'

Trisha Martyn was the school Head of Games this year. Part of the training programme for the young squad was to play against a sevens team picked from Trebizon's hockey First Eleven. No opposition they came up against in the Under-15s national tournament would beat that!

They had a fierce, gruelling game that afternoon and loved every minute of it. Although only a substitute, Rebecca changed in regularly. She was as fast and fit as anybody, but her stickwork was not up to the same standard as the best players in the squad.

The seniors beat them 7–2. It was quite respectable, thanks mainly to some good saves under pressure by Jenny in goal, and some marvellously versatile play by Tish and Laura who set up both the goals that Eleanor scored.

'Well done,' said Trisha Martyn afterwards.

Tish looked pleased. Rebecca knew that both Tish and Laura hoped to equal Joss's record and get a place in the First Eleven before they were fifteen. They were both already in the school's Second Eleven. It would have to happen this term, if it were going to!

'We must try Jenny in that full-back position soon,' Tish said to Laura, after they'd all had showers back in the sports centre. Beth Bingley's performance with the Clifford Cats had more significance after a high-powered game. 'You remember? What Joss was talking about? The more I think about it, the more I like it.'

'We couldn't leave an empty goal today!' laughed Laura. 'It would never have worked.'

'Oh, no, not today,' agreed Tish.

'We'll rake up a few more players, just for some practice games. Verity would like to help,' suggested Laura. 'It looks as though the weather's getting better now. We'll get going with some more seven-a-side games, and then we can try that with Jenny.'

'She'll need practice,' said Tish. 'But it'll be so good if it works. It gives you an extra player!'

'D'you know, I've only ever seen Jenny play in goal,' said Laura.

After tea, Rebecca sat down and wrote a letter to Robbie at last. She'd been thinking for some time about how to word it:

*Dear Robbie*

*Thanks for the brooch. It's beautiful. It was very exciting when I won at Birmingham, as you can imagine.*

*I've put off writing this note because I also want to say thank you for all the help you gave me last year. Especially with my serve. You really helped.*

*But if I say that, it gives the impression that I think I'm really good now and I'm not sure if I am. Joss doesn't think so. (And she should know!) We shall just have to see – but thanks anyway.*

*I hope you're winning all your rugby matches and Tish tells me you're working very hard this term for exams. I'll phone you when they're all over and see how you got on.*

*Love, Rebecca*

She put it in an envelope and managed to catch Curly, just as Mara was seeing him off downstairs. They'd been singing together in a scratch choir that met on Sunday afternoons and he'd stayed on to tea. Curly was two years younger than Robbie, but they were both in Syon House.

'Can you put this in Robbie Anderson's pigeon-hole, please?'

'Sure,' said Curly.

Mara and Rebecca walked back upstairs together. Mara glanced at Rebecca, putting her head on one side, questioningly. 'You are going to make it up?'

Rebecca smiled and shook her head. 'No,' she said. Then, when Mara looked disappointed, she added: 'Well, maybe, sometime.'

When the six returned to Court House after breakfast on Monday morning, the postman had been.

'It's arrived!' cried Rebecca snatching down from the mail board a familiar-looking buff envelope. 'Hey! It looks as though it's been half way round England.'

Then, as she looked at the front of the envelope carefully, she burst out laughing.

'Oh, so that's why it's taken so long. How stupid of me! How could I have been such a fool!'

It was, sure enough, the stamped addressed envelope that she'd sent to London with her results sheet, originally. But she'd absent-mindedly written on it her grandmother's address in Gloucestershire! Her gran had crossed it all out and written PLEASE FORWARD (squiggles) 'Trebizon' – and judging by postmarks it had been somewhere else first. Old Mrs Mason's handwriting was not very easy to read.

'Well, now it's here, open it!' exclaimed Tish.

'Yes, come on, Rebecca!' said Margot. They were all pressing round.

Rebecca tore open the sealed envelope, excitedly. 'It feels thick!' she said. Then she pulled out some sheets of paper and unfolded them. They were stapled together in the corner.

It said at the top of the first sheet: LTA COMPUTER RANKING – BWTA SYSTEM.

Then GIRLS UNDER-16, with the date of the Results period the ranking referred to.

It gave the current British junior ranking from one to one hundred and twenty-eight for girls aged sixteen and under. The columns from left to right were headed:

Ranking position/name/computer registration number/ county/date of birth/category/ total tournament points/total wins/number of tournaments represented/number of tournaments won/best four events.

It was all very mathematical!

But only two columns mattered to Rebecca right now – the first two – ranking number, followed by name!

'Come on!' said Sue, craning her neck.

'Give me a chance!' laughed Rebecca. 'I'm just looking.' It was a sea of names and numbers!

The rankings ran to four pages in all. Rebecca flicked over the first page, 1–42, immediately – and then the second page, 43–84, equally quickly. Not much point in looking at those. This would be her, the third page, rankings 85–126. She ran her eye down the column of names, then up again, then down again.

'Oh,' she said. Her name wasn't there.

The two bottom rankings ran over on to the fourth page. 127 and 128 had a page to themselves. She looked. But she wasn't either of those.

'I can't find my name,' she said wryly. 'I don't seem to have made the Under-16 rankings after all.

But Mrs Ericson said I would!'

'You haven't even looked at the first two pages!' exclaimed Tish. She grabbed the wadge of paper from Rebecca and flicked back to the second page.

'Here you are, you idiot! Number 65!'

'65!' cried Rebecca in delight. 'Where – show me?'

She stared at the entry: 65 *Mason, Rebecca*.

'65!' she repeated.

'Hey!' said Tish. She'd realised, too. 'Fiona *said* 65.'

They all looked at one another in surprise. 'What an incredible coincidence!' laughed Sue.

'She also said 126,' grinned Margot.

'Just hedging her bets,' said Elf.

But Rebecca was riffling through the papers, suddenly looking very excited. 'How odd! There's some more sheets underneath, another set of rankings. GIRLS UNDER 18. They've sent me those as well. Surely –'

'You must be in them!' cried Tish in triumph.

'I don't believe it,' said Rebecca, turning the pages.

But then the paper trembled.

'Yes. I'm here.'

'What number?' asked Tish curiously. 'Come on, what's your under-18 ranking then?'

Rebecca was silent.

Standing back, drawing away from the group, Mara's eyes were wide and startled.

'Come on, Rebecca!' Elf whispered. 'Tell us.'

'You'd better look for yourselves,' said Rebecca and passed the sheets round. 'I can see you're all agog!'

It was there, right at the bottom of the third page:

126 Mason, Rebecca.

So Fiona had been right after all!

There was a silence, to be broken by Tish.

'Very impressive,' she said.

'What – me or Fiona?' asked Rebecca, drily.

'Both.'

# EIGHT
## Shiver Down the Spine

'Fiona!' whispered Rebecca during registration.

It was a few minutes later. The six had arrived at the IV Alpha form room, which was on the first floor of old school, panting and out of breath. They were only just in time – Miss Maggs was about to call the register!

'Yes?' whispered Fiona. She could see that Rebecca looked flushed and elated.

'Congratulations!' exclaimed Rebecca. 'My computer ranking's just come – and you were right. I *have* got two numbers and they were the ones you said!'

'Really?' A pleased smile spread slowly across Fiona's placid face. She mouthed: 'Oh, good! And are you pleased, Rebecca?'

'Pleased? I'm walking on air!' whispered Rebecca. She was also deeply mystified.

'Stop talking, over by the window there!' rapped Miss Maggs.

'Sorry, Miss Maggs,' murmured Rebecca, and that was that.

Within an hour the Trebizon grapevine was at work and the news spread around the whole of the Fourth Year.

Fiona Freeman had done a fortune-telling act at Elizabeth Kendall's birthday party and foretold the future! She really had – no joke! She'd told Rebecca Mason what her computer rankings were going to be! She'd got both the numbers right! Rebecca's letter had only arrived this morning – but Fiona had seen the numbers in her crystal ball last Friday. She definitely *had* – there were witnesses to prove it!

If Fiona had needed a success, she now had one. A sensational success at that. She was famous! She was the centre of attention on her dinner table.

In fact people were so amazed that she had to try to calm them down a bit!

'How did you do it, Fiona?'

'How did you *do* it, Fiona?'

– asked Sarah and Ruth Nathan in almost the same breath.

'Have you really got the gift of second sight?' exclaimed Debbie Rickard. 'Really?'

'Of course she has!' said Roberta Jones. 'Oh, Fiona – there's something I'm desperate to know. I'm dying to know what Daddy's going to give me for my birthday. Will you look in your crystal ball, *please*?'

'I've got at least three things I'm desperate to know!' exclaimed Jane Ford. 'Give me a go first, Fiona!'

'No, me!' said Helena King.

Fiona was inundated with requests but just sat there placidly and finally she said:

'I can't just do it to order. I've got to feel the right vibrations.'

'Tell us when you get them!'

'I will,' said Fiona. 'But you mustn't keep on about it. It's not something I get very often.' She sounded slightly irritable. 'So let's shut up about it now.'

'Sorry, Fiona.'

'We won't say another word.'

Somebody so gifted, sitting amongst them!

To think they'd hardly noticed her to start with. Obviously she was going to be a bit temperamental, with a gift like that. Like poets and their muse. Maybe she had mystic blood in her? She must have!

'Have another helping of bakewell tart, Fiona,' said Elizabeth Fichumi, who was the head of table this term.

'It's the last piece,' demurred the new girl.

'We don't mind! You have it!' they all chorused.

'Thanks,' said Fiona, looking pleased. She picked it up and stuffed it in her mouth.

As for the six friends in Court House, their views on Fiona were divided.

They didn't take all their lessons together, being in different sets for some subjects and doing various GCSE options anyway, but they discussed it all when they got together at lunch time and again at tea time. When they met up back in the rooms at Court House later, they discussed it yet again. Tish and Rebecca went up and flopped on their beds after another session in the gym, while Sue was only coming back to collect her violin. She had to go on to a music lesson soon. The other three had been doing their prep.

'It's ESP, it must be,' grinned Tish, lying on her back and staring at the ceiling. 'She's got the force! Isn't it exciting!'

'Don't say that,' said Mara, giving a little shudder. 'It gives me the creeps!'

'She might have just guessed,' said Sue. She was kneeling on her bed, opening up her violin case. 'Though the mathematical odds against getting *both* numbers correct must be 100–1.'

'100–1?' scoffed Tish. 'Don't be daft, Sue. The odds are $128^2$–1, and I can tell you what that is because I worked it out during history this morning. It's 16384–1.'

'What, without a calculator?' asked Rebecca admiringly.

'I don't believe it!' said Mara heatedly. She looked upset.

'Oh, I can assure you –' began Tish. 'Here, Elf, chuck over your calculator and I'll prove it –'

'No!' Mara cut in. 'I mean I don't believe in ET!'

'Not ET, Mara!' laughed Rebecca. 'That's Extra-Terrestial. ESP. Extra Sensory Perception!'

'ET – ESP – who cares! I don't believe in it,' said Mara. She added darkly: '*She cheated somehow.*'

'But how – how –?' asked Margot.

'I know!' exclaimed Elf. 'Maybe she rang up London and got the rankings over the telephone!'

'They wouldn't have given them to her, I'm sure,' said Rebecca. She frowned.

'Not even if she pretended to be you?' propounded Mara.

'No.' Rebecca shook her head. 'I'm sure they don't give them over the phone.'

'In any case,' said Tish, 'why should she go to such fantastic lengths?'

'I know then – maybe she broke into Miss Willis's office or something and found out all Rebecca's results since October and then got a calculator –' babbled Elf '– and then maybe, somehow, she managed to . . .' Her voice trailed feebly away. 'Work them out for herself?'

'Oh, Elf!' laughed Rebecca. 'She'd have needed everybody's results. Everybody in the whole country!'

'And you're a crack pot!' giggled Tish.

'I *still* think she's a phoney,' glowered Mara, refusing to find any of this amusing.

Then suddenly Sue scraped the bow over the strings of her violin and said:

'Blast!'

'What's the matter?' asked Margot.

'Well, listen!'

She bowed the strings much harder this time.

It was a rough, raucous sound and they put their hands to their ears.

'I meant to get some new rosin today!' exclaimed Sue. 'Now I'll have to borrow Mrs Costello's again.'

'Oh, Sue!' scolded Elf. 'You've been looking for that rosin for days –'

'ROSIN!' exclaimed Tish, sitting bolt upright on the bed.

'Fiona!' remembered Rebecca.

'Radiator!' added Sue. Her eyes narrowed behind her spectacles. 'She saw it in her crystal ball, didn't she? Behind a radiator.'

'And you haven't even looked?' said Tish.

'Well, it was too late after the party,' confessed Sue, 'and anyway, there's a hundred radiators –'

'– and anyway, we forgot about it!' laughed Tish. She bounced along the bed on her knees until she reached the radiator, which ended just by her headboard. 'I'll have a squint–'

Tish twisted her face into horrible contortions, trying to squint down behind the radiator.

'We could at least look at the one in our room!' she was saying.

'Oh, don't bother, Tish,' said Mara. She was biting her lip nervously. 'Leave it.'

'Can you see anything?' asked Rebecca, intrigued.

'I – I – think – I can see – well – *something*. Here, pass me a ruler, somebody.'

Margot obliged.

Tish jiggled and poked with the ruler. 'It's touching something! It's moving –'

Then –

PLOP!

Mara gasped out loud and they all stared in amazement as a little red box dropped down from behind the radiator and landed on the floor. Its lid flew off.

'*My rosin!*' exclaimed Sue.

'Good heavens,' said Rebecca. A little bit of a shiver ran up and down her spine. 'How *does* she do it?'

Sue touched the rosin box gingerly with the toe of her shoe. Mara backed away from it, as though it were a tarantula. Then Sue bent and picked it up.

'Yes, this is mine all right. Well, what an amazing thing.'

'You see, Mara?' Tish laughed in delight. 'Now are you convinced?'

'No!' Mara stamped her foot in rage. She looked tearful.

She walked over to the door.

'I'm going downstairs to watch TV. I don't understand what is happening – not yet. But I shall think about it very hard! She is trying to frighten us –'

'Oh, Mara, I'm sure she isn't trying to do *that* –' protested Tish.

'Well, I don't believe she has magic ESP powers –

I don't know how she does all these funny things – but I shall make it my business to find out!' Mara opened the door and peered out into the corridor, as though nervous at what she might see out there. Then she turned back to them, an angry light in her brown eyes.

'And when I have found out, I shall expose her!'

She went out and slammed the door behind her.

There was an uncomfortable silence. They hated it when Mara got upset. Then Sue looked at her watch.

'I'm late for my lesson. I'd better run! I'll take this with me and do it over there.' She put the rosin into its small compartment inside the violin case, then started to slacken her bow before packing it.

'And I'd better go and ring Mrs Ericson!' exclaimed Rebecca.

'Whatever for?' asked Tish.

'Why d'you think?' asked Rebecca in surprise. 'It's gone six o'clock – she'll be home now. I'm supposed to ring her as soon as I've got my ranking!'

'Of course,' mumbled Tish.

'It'll be really exciting to hear what she has to say, Rebecca!' said Elf, the first to recover. 'You've done so fantastically well.'

'Brilliantly,' added Sue.

But Rebecca wasn't fooled. They'd forgotten. They'd even forgotten to congratulate her this morning. The simple truth was that her triumph had been rather overshadowed by Fiona's.

In different circumstances, Rebecca knew that her friends would all have made a great fuss of her today. But somehow it was Fiona Freeman who'd occupied the centre of the stage!

Rebecca couldn't help feeling a little disappointed. When, in fact, she passed Fiona coming up the stairs just as she was going down to phone, she returned her enthusiastic 'Hello, Rebecca!' with a slightly cool smile.

She didn't even pause to tell her about the rosin.

Fiona carried on upstairs then wandered along to her room, musing. She'd been thinking of watching TV downstairs, but she'd got such a cold stare from Mara Leonodis when she'd ventured to go in there that she'd changed her mind! Now Rebecca looked a bit distant, too.

In fact Rebecca's mild dejection was to vanish instantly when she got through to the coach with her news.

'Wonderful, Rebecca! I'm overjoyed! To have got

into the Under-18 rankings as well! Even better than I expected! You had such consistently good results last term – and some of the people you beat in the summer were in the older age group – and then the win at Birmingham. It's all gone into the computer! You've got the sort of ranking you deserve now, you've worked so hard!'

'I – I couldn't quite believe my eyes when I saw it,' said Rebecca shyly, gripping the telephone hard. 'Will I play for the Under 16s now, Mrs Ericson?'

'Virtually certain. There's a selectors' meeting Thursday. And I'm sure you'll be given some senior matches as well! But in any case, I think we should meet and make plans – urgently.'

'Plans?' said Rebecca, intrigued.

'Yes. Look, this is a rather crackly line, Rebecca. I'll be very near Trebizon on Friday. We can all meet then. I'll arrange a meeting with Greta Darling, and I'll see you at school. We can talk then.'

The money was running out and they said hurried goodbyes. Rebecca replaced the receiver.

What did Mrs Ericson want to meet about on Friday? What was urgent?

Rebecca suddenly felt rather excited.

# NINE
## Matters Unresolved

The rain clouds of the previous week did not reappear and some fine weather set in. There were frosty snaps overnight, dusting the hockey pitches with white and lightly stiffening each blade of grass. But the morning sun was quite warm for January, melting the frost, turning the hockey pitches green again, fit to play on by the lunch hour. The afternoon sunsets were getting later, too, giving more than an hour of daylight after lessons had finished each day.

So now the Tigers – as everyone began to call them – could get out of doors and start practising in earnest, twice a day if necessary.

Verity Williams, Laura's friend in Tavistock, got up a rival seven called the Cubs for them to practise against. It was composed of the best Third

Eleven players – Roberta Jones, Joanne Thompson, Marjorie Spar, Judy Sharp and Verity herself. Plus Sheila Cummings, Wanda Gorski and Rebecca – who were, of course, substitutes in the Tigers squad, not in the side proper. However, Wanda and Rebecca, both being forwards, took it in turns to play for the Tigers – because there was a permanent gap in the forward line-up with Joss away in America.

Sometimes Tish, who was so good that she could afford to do it, gave Sheila her sweeper's position in the Tigers and played happily for the Cubs in Sheila's place.

It was important that the three substitutes, as members of the squad, should get plenty of experience of playing with their own side. They'd be needed on the day!

Rebecca found those games exhilarating, especially when playing for the Tigers. They could all run like hares, beating the Cubs! But both sides were good, the cream of Trebizon's Middle School talent – who as juniors had been the squad to win the West of England Junior Gold Cup.

She was looking forward to the day when the new strip would arrive and was longing to wear it. She was determined to make her tackling more positive and her passes more accurate, to bring her stickwork up to the standard of some of the others. It wasn't going to be enough just to be very fit and a fast runner, though of course that helped!

'Well done,' said Miss Jacobs on the Thursday. She'd now been appointed as the Tigers' coach and joined them when she could. 'But remember, you've only got six players in effect and there's a lot of ground to cover. Aba and Laura, you could play forward more than you do. Don't think of yourselves as backs, come up to the attack whenever you can. You're both champion runners, you've got all the speed you need to race back and defend when you have to. Aba, you're getting a lot of possession – but practise hitting the ball really hard, getting it clear of your circle, don't poke at it.' She smiled then. 'I must say, it's all working well.'

Later she confided to Laura and Tish:

'But I didn't think it was a good idea to take Jenny out of goal and play her as a full-back. You can only risk those tactics when you have a girl who'll *burst* into play, using her feet and her stick with equal effect, and really *scatter* the opposition before they can get near the goal. Someone who can intimidate them almost. And she needs a good turn of speed to get back into the goalmouth and defend if anything goes wrong!'

'But Joss Vining put us on to it!' protested Tish. 'You've as good as got an extra player with someone like that.'

'We'd like to persevere with Jenny, Miss Jacobs,' said Laura quietly. 'On the day of the tournament I'd like to be able to switch her around, depending on who we're playing against. Sometimes in goal, sometimes not. It could make all the difference to how well we do! A school like Queensbury is bound to have a keeper they can bring forward as full-back when they need to.'

'Yes, but I don't think *you* have,' said Miss Jacobs lightly. 'Jenny's outstanding in goal and, if it were up to me, I'd leave it at that. But then – you're the team's captain, Laura, so I must keep quiet, mustn't I?'

'Yes!' said Tish cheekily. Miss Jacobs laughed.

At Trebizon girls were expected to take decisions from an early age, take responsibility for them – and learn by their mistakes if things went wrong.

'Jenny just needs time to adapt, Miss Jacobs,' said Laura. 'There's a lot of time.'

But secretly both she and Tish were uneasy.

So was Jenny.

Rebecca tapped on the door of her room on the Thursday evening. She'd at last finished rewriting the piece that Jenny, as Magazine Officer, had submitted to *The Trebizon Journal* from the Fourth Year. 'The Tournament I Never Thought I'd Win – by R. Mason.' The magazine meeting had approved it when they'd read it but Lady Edwina Burton, who was this year's editor of *The Journal*, had sent it back for cutting. Rebecca had never liked the titled prefect very much, but on reflection she'd had to admit to herself that the piece suffered from being too wordy and tentative. She hadn't been feeling buoyant about her tennis, anyway, when she'd written it – and it showed.

Now she'd cut it in places and revised it in others. She felt it was much better.

'Jenny?' Rebecca opened the door and went in.

The room was on the opposite side of the corridor from theirs, and its windows overlooked the front. There was no sign of Elizabeth. Jenny was standing by the far window, gazing moodily out into the darkness.

'I've brought the piece,' said Rebecca, laying it down on Jenny's bed. 'What's wrong?'

'Oh, I'm fed up,' said Jenny. 'I was hopeless today, wasn't I?'

She turned and gazed at Rebecca.

'Come on, be honest.'

Rebecca smiled.

'Well, you're not as good at full-back as you are in goal, if that's what you mean,' she said. 'But there's no point in worrying about it! If it doesn't work out, Laura will just have to give up the idea.'

'But she's so keen on it!' Jenny blurted out. 'So's Tish.'

'Oh, they'd never even have *thought* of it if we hadn't gone to Joss's for the weekend. They'd never have known anything about it!' Rebecca pointed out. 'It can't be that important.'

'You know what I'm beginning to wish?' said Jenny, with feeling. 'I'm beginning to wish we'd never gone to Joss's.'

'It's funny you should say that,' replied Rebecca. 'I sometimes have that feeling myself.'

As she lay in bed that night, gazing up at the ceiling, Rebecca reflected that it was something difficult to shake off – lurking like a small shadow – the memory of Joss's crushing words. She was still deeply mystified by Joss's attitude that day. It had seemed so out of character.

Sue was convinced that Joss was getting big-headed. And Jenny wasn't too thrilled with her, either. But could Joss really have changed? Rebecca didn't think so.

It was unresolved.

But it was Friday tomorrow! The meeting between Mrs Ericson and Miss Darling and herself had now been arranged, for half-past three. Miss Willis was going to come along, too. They were all going to have tea and biscuits in Mrs Barrington's sitting room.

'And the meeting's going to be about me!' thought Rebecca, in wonder.

She banished the small lurking shadow from her mind.

Whatever Joss might say, she had no intention of giving up her tennis ambitions now!

Even if it *was* the hockey term.

Something else was unresolved. Mara was still very unhappy about having lost her butterfly hair slide.

She'd been to Lost Property several times. She kept asking people if they'd seen it. She'd even offered some of the juniors a small reward if they found it – and they'd been out scouring the grounds at lunch time. The whole thing was turning into a saga which was rather ridiculous when one considered that the slide had only cost fifty pence in the first place. But –

'It's precious, Rebecca. The day Curly bought it for me was very special. We made a secret pact that day! You do understand? Besides, we're going down town on Saturday afternoon, Curly and I, and it goes with my new red top.'

Rebecca understood perfectly. She had a precious talisman of her own, sitting in her bedside locker.

She hadn't yet been able to bring herself to wear the brooch that Robbie had given her, but it gave her an odd feeling of happiness and security to know that it was there.

Even so, Mara was getting to be a bit of a bore about the slide.

'I must find it!' she said, the moment she climbed out of bed on Friday morning. 'It's brought me bad luck, losing it! Yesterday the nib of my fountain pen broke and the day before the heel came off my shoe!'

'Oh, don't be so superstitious, Mara,' said Sue, groping for her spectacles.

'Why don't you ask Fiona to look in the crystal ball?' grunted Tish sleepily. 'She'll find it for you!'

The news of Fiona's success in locating Sue's rosin had, of course, spread. All week she'd had a stream of requests to use her unearthly powers, especially from the juniors.

'I've lost my left hockey shoe, Fiona. It's black and the lace is broken – my name's written inside it with purple felt-tip.'

'Please find my recorder for me, Fiona. It's desperate.'

And apparently, on Wednesday, Fiona had had another success. She'd been able to tell little Sarah

Butters that her new plimsolls were being worn by another girl in the First Year, and sure enough it had turned out to be true.

But on Friday morning the very mention of Fiona's name was enough to upset Mara.

'I shall ask her nothing. No fear! It is stupid to encourage her. She is a menace, that girl!'

'Oh, let her enjoy herself,' said Tish.

But Mara had no intention of letting Fiona enjoy herself.

In fact, Mara was beginning to upset Fiona quite as much as the other way round.

She was going around saying to people that Fiona didn't have the gift of second sight at all and that she must have found out Rebecca's computer ranking by some kind of trick. She must have telephoned London – disguised her voice and pretended to be Rebecca – and been given the rankings over the phone!

Well Fiona denied it, of course. Mara was *quite wrong* about that.

But she didn't like it. She couldn't have Mara going around saying things like that!

Also, she could have sworn that she'd seen Mara following her around once or twice.

It was most unnerving. She didn't want Mara as an enemy. She wanted to make friends in Court House, not enemies.

There was nothing for it but to concentrate hard, draw deeply on her resources and convince Mara once and for all. Then, surely, she would be much more friendly?

# TEN
## Getting the Vibrations

Rebecca had washed, changed and tidied up, ready for the meeting at half-past three. She'd felt hot and sticky after an hour's tennis coaching with Miss Darling, who'd told her not to be late for the meeting. Now she groped in her locker until she found the brooch that Robbie had given her, took it out, looked at it – and decided to pin it on. Would it bring her luck? She'd pin it somewhere unobtrusive, so that nobody could see it. Under the lapel of her blazer, that would do.

She was in the room alone. Everybody seemed to be out. Sue was back in the school's Third Eleven – at centre-forward. They'd all waved her off after lunch – the team was playing Caxton High, away. Friday was a games afternoon this term and Rebecca had last seen Tish over on north pitch, getting some coaching with the rest of the Second Eleven. The other three had opted for swimming and were presumably down in the swimming pool at the sports centre.

Laura had cancelled after-school hockey practice today – half the Tigers were away, playing for the Third Eleven. So Rebecca was pleased that the meeting about her tennis wasn't going to interfere with that.

Just as she was pinning on the brooch, the door flew open and Tish bounded in.

'Rebeck!'

'Yes?' She quickly fumbled the clasp shut (though not quite shut) and turned round, furious with herself because she was blushing slightly. 'Oh, hello, Tish.'

'What sort of car has your coach got? Is it a small yellow one?'

'Yes!'

'Then she's here. It's parked outside Mrs Barry's front door. You'd better hurry.'

'Oh, thanks.' Rebecca gave her hair a last pat and walked towards the door.

'Good luck!' said Tish. 'I'm dying to hear all about it.'

'Where will you be?' asked Rebecca.

'I'm going for a run – tide's out. Probably to the far side of Mulberry Cove and back. I'll be down on the beach. I've got a bit of news, too!'

'See you there then,' said Rebecca. 'I won't be long. Apparently Mrs Ericson's only got a few minutes. See you, Tish!'

She hurried downstairs, then out of the front door and round the corner. Mr and Mrs Barrington lived in a private wing of Court House and had their own separate entrance at the side. Sure enough, the familiar yellow car was there – and Mrs Barry's front door was open. She was expected.

'We're in the sitting room, Rebecca!' called Miss Willis, as she entered the hall.

It was a comfortable room with a piano in one corner, the loose covers on the sofa and armchairs a faded red and white chintz material, cheerful and homely. Miss Willis, Mrs Ericson, Mrs Barrington and Miss Darling were all seated around a low glass-topped table. On it Mrs Barry had placed a silver teapot and milk jug, cups and saucers of delicate porcelain and a plate of chocolate digestive biscuits.

'Tea, Rebecca?' asked the House Mistress.

'Yes, please!' said Rebecca. She stared at the table.

The best tea things *and* chocolate digestive biscuits. Always reserved for special occasions! So this *was* special – it really was. Important. About her!

And Mrs Ericson, she noticed, had various sheets of paper spread out on the sofa beside her – tournament entry forms, that sort of thing.

'We've got to keep this brief, Rebecca. Do sit down,' said Miss Willis with a pleasant smile. 'I'm sure you'll be delighted to know that Mrs Ericson thinks you have a sporting chance of being accepted for the Prudential hard courts this year – you know, the Under-16 at Edgbaston in the Easter holidays.'

Rebecca *did* know about the Prudential. She sat down with a bump!

'But that's a national event!' she exclaimed, feeling weak at the knees. 'Only the top juniors get accepted for that.'

'The top sixty, roughly,' said Mrs Ericson, in a matter-of-fact way. 'The top sixty girls in your age group. Your computer ranking's sixty-five at the moment. Your application form needn't go in until the beginning of March. If you can get some good results in the next few weeks and earn yourself some more tournament points, that'll be taken into account. In effect, you can up your ranking!

So we've been discussing ways you can try to do it.'

She shuffled through the papers she'd brought. It was all very businesslike.

'The county has put you in for a senior match tomorrow – it's away, but Miss Darling has kindly offered to drive you. That could earn you some points. And there are three quite useful tournaments coming up – they'll give you the chance to play girls above you on the computer. Rita Sullivan for instance, you really must beat her. And Rachel Cathcart . . .'

Rebecca sat there in silence, drinking her tea, her head spinning a little, as the four women around her in brisk but kindly tones organised her tennis programme for the next few weeks. It could be fitted into the school timetable quite easily – transport was the main problem. Some of the venues were awkward by train, it was necessary for her to be taken by car.

Rebecca knew it was a disadvantage, and one that she was beginning to notice more and more, that her parents were stationed abroad. Most of the other competitive young players that she saw at tournaments were blessed with 'tennis parents', devoted mums and dads, who spent a large part of their lives getting their children to important matches in various parts of the country.

But Mrs Ericson and these three members of staff were determined that she shouldn't suffer in any way. She saw them consulting their diaries, making notes, agreeing to take it in turns. She heard Greta Darling, stiff and unsmiling, but really quite fond of Rebecca, say at one point: *'In loco parentis.* It's the least we can do.'

*In place of parents!* Trebizon. Rebecca was touched by that.

And so it was all settled. The last of the three tournaments was at Bristol, over half-term, so she wouldn't be able to go to her gran's. Mrs Barry was going to take her to that one. It would be a chance to earn some big points just before her application went in. Gran would understand.

Before she was dismissed, Rebecca managed to find her voice and ask one or two really important questions.

'Did the selectors meet? Am I in the county team?'

'Of course!' said Mrs Ericson 'You've been put in the Under-16 team at number three.'

'How many points will I have to earn to get

accepted for the Prudential?'

'That depends entirely on how well your rivals are doing! The girls just above you.'

And then, just before she left the room, she remembered –

'When is it? It won't clash with the seven-a-sides, will it?'

'Not at all,' laughed Miss Willis. 'It's a fortnight later. Oh, Rebecca, you do want to have your cake and eat it!'

Rebecca smiled. It was true. How awful if the two things had clashed!

'You can't spend too much time playing hockey, though,' Mrs Ericson warned her. 'Not in the long term! Not even in the short term. Not if you want to go to Eastbourne in August!'

Rebecca was halfway to the door. She stopped dead. Eastbourne! *The* national junior tournament in Britain. In August – when her parents would be home on leave!

'Is – is there the slightest chance of that?' she asked, her mouth feeling dry.

'Certainly there's a chance,' said Mrs Ericson cautiously. 'But let's see how we go. Let's see if we make the Prudential first, shall we?'

Rebecca nodded eagerly, then left the room. Instinctively she touched her crossed tennis rackets pinned under her lapel. It *had* brought her luck, wearing Robbie's brooch.

She ran all the way to the beach to find Tish.

'Marvellous, Rebecca!' said Tish. 'I can't get over it.'

The two girls were sitting on top of one of the sand dunes, gazing across Trebizon Bay. Rebecca turned and looked at Tish.

'You're not doing too badly yourself!' she exclaimed.

It seemed that Tish was going to be given a trial for the school's First Eleven! The news had been broken to her and Laura during coaching that afternoon. They were both down for first team trials. Miss Jacobs had noticed how brilliantly they'd both been playing during sevens practices this week and had had a word with Trisha Martyn about it.

The girls sat in silence and drank in the scene. The tide was far out and the sand seemed to stretch as far as the eye could see. The bay was totally deserted except for the distant figure of a man, one of the townspeople, walking his dog along the shore. He was as small as a Lowry pinman against the vast backcloth of sky and sand and rolling sea which, towards the far horizon, was tinged silver and red by a spectacular winter sunset.

They looked up when they heard a droning sound, coming from inland, and saw a flash of silver as an airliner passed overhead. It was climbing steadily, heading westwards into the sunset.

'I wonder if it's going to the States?' said Tish, with a smile.

'I wonder!' replied Rebecca.

They watched as it got tinier and tinier and then disappeared over the horizon.

It made them think of Joss Vining.

'Won't it be fun if you can equal Joss's record?' said Rebecca, after a while. 'Play for the first team before you're fifteen!'

Tish nodded. She brought her knees up to her chin and rested it there, an excited light in her brown eyes as she stared out to sea. 'They're touring Holland after Easter,' she said. Then she added, 'If you manage to get accepted for the Prudential, will Joss be playing there? I mean, she'll be back, won't she?'

Rebecca shook her head.

'No, she wouldn't be allowed to enter. Not when

she's been abroad for a whole year. Of course, she'll be all right by August. She'll have a British ranking again by then. She can play at Eastbourne.'

'She went to Eastbourne when she was only thirteen, didn't she?' commented Tish.

Rebecca nodded. The tiny shadow was back, just for a moment. Tish seemed to read her mind:

'I don't know why she had to be so downbeat towards you, Rebecca. Wasn't that odd! Well, I'm sure she'll begin to think differently when she comes back and hears the news.'

'What news?' laughed Rebecca. 'There isn't any news yet. Not by Joss's standards!'

'But there's going to be!' grinned Tish. 'You've got to get accepted for the Prudential. And then, after that – Eastbourne!'

Rebecca looked thoughtful.

'I must say . . .' She picked up a handful of sand and let it run through her fingers.

'What?'

'It would be rather nice, wouldn't it?' said Rebecca. 'It would be rather nice to prove Joss wrong. I'd like to give her a surprise!'

That was her ambition now.

Making their way back to school from the beach, they met Fiona Freeman at the little wicket gate that led into the copse at the back of Juniper House. They could hear the tea bell ringing, up on the campus somewhere! They were late!

'Been for a run, Fiona?' asked Tish, in surprise.

The big girl was wearing a tracksuit and looked somewhat out of breath. There was a lot of colour in her cheeks and she seemed elated about something. She'd come from the direction of the town beach.

'Not a run exactly,' said Fiona mysteriously. 'Just been enjoying myself. Am I *hungry*!'

'Aren't we all!' exclaimed Rebecca. The chocolate digestives already seemed an age away. 'Come on, there's the second bell. We'd better hurry.'

As they jogged up the footpath towards the main school buildings, Rebecca caught a delicious whiff of something from the direction of the kitchens. 'Fish and chips!'

'Hurray!' said Fiona, and charged past them.

Running powerfully, she shot ahead of them and disappeared round the corner.

'What's she been doing to get so hungry?' asked Rebecca in surprise.

Up to this moment Fiona had shown no signs

whatsoever of being the outdoor type, playing netball under duress during games lessons but otherwise tending to stay in the warm as much as possible.

'She looked to me as though she'd been down on the wet part of the sands, making dams or something with her bare hands,' laughed Tish. 'Did you see her trainers? They were filthy. So were her hands!'

'Well, let's hope she remembers to wash them,' smiled Rebecca. 'At least she's on another table!'

First thing on Saturday morning the rest of the six crowded round Rebecca, patting her on the back and shoulders.

'Good luck!'

'Off you go!'

Miss Darling had come to pick her up and was parked downstairs, in the front, sounding the horn. Jenny had rushed through and told them.

'Got everything, Rebecca?' asked Tish. 'Mustn't keep the Dread waiting!'

It was going to be a great day in Rebecca's life. Representing the county in a senior match! This was really throwing her in at the deep end. The fixture was against the next county but one, on covered courts, and the drive alone would take nearly three hours.

'I *think* I've got everything,' said Rebecca. She'd packed her sports grip and had stuffed Biffy, her teddy bear mascot, inside. She'd got both her rackets and some spare socks, sweat bands, talcum powder, the new tennis dress she'd ordered from that catalogue at Christmas. But her eyes darted to her blazer, lying on the end of the bed. Robbie's brooch! 'I'll just take my blazer,' she said quickly, and rushed back and snatched it up.

'What do you want your blazer for?' laughed Sue.

Then they shepherded her down the stairs, all in a bunch.

In the hall, Rebecca glanced swiftly at the mail board. She always did. She wasn't really expecting anything. She'd written to Robbie but there was no reason for him to write back. It was unreasonable of her to think he might! But she always looked, just in case.

Nothing today.

*Honnkkkk!*

She ran outside and climbed into the car. 'Good morning, Rebecca.'

They were off.

It was a long, exhausting – and exhilarating! – day for Rebecca.

Only one small thing clouded it. Just before she got out of the car at their destination, she leant over to the back seat and groped under the lapel of her blazer for Robbie's brooch. It wasn't there! 'I'm getting absent-minded!' thought Rebecca. 'I can't remember taking it off last night and putting it back in my locker. But I must have done, mustn't I?' She'd been so looking forward to pinning it on her new tennis dress!

'Come on Rebecca. You won't need your blazer. Leave it in the car. Just bring your grip. I've got your rackets.'

'Yes, Miss Darling.'

But Rebecca won one of her two matches!

She'd only been given this chance to play in the senior side because some of the regular players had flu. Nobody was expecting too much of her. The odd thing was that she lost the easier match and won the more difficult one, which was against another underage player, an outstanding fifteen-year-old, called Deborah Bond.

'I hope you're not going to turn into one of those competitors who can only play their best when they come from behind!' commented Miss Darling, on the journey back. Secretly she was delighted with Rebecca's performance – she'd been a set down and 3–4 down in the second set before levelling at 4-all and then going on to win the second and third sets.

'I suddenly realised that she's a long way above me on the computer and it might be a good thing to beat her!' said Rebecca truthfully. 'So I pulled all the stops out.'

'You certainly ran her into the ground. You're very fit these days, Rebecca.'

But by the time they got back on the Saturday evening, Rebecca was also very tired!

She'd had a bath as soon as she got back. By nine o'clock – sitting in the little Common Room in her dressing gown – it was all she could do to keep her eyes open. They were all in their pyjamas (except for Sue who was playing her violin at a charity concert in the town) and Mara had insisted on making some cocoa.

'Poor Rebecca – you look so sleepy! Here, drink your cocoa up and then you must go to bed!'

'Thanks, Mara.'

The five of them sat around in their night things. They'd just finished off their cocoa and were talking about nothing in particular, when they suddenly heard footsteps padding along the corridor.

'Mara!' a voice called.

The door burst open and Fiona stood there in her dressing gown, flushed with excitement. She'd been running.

'What's wrong?' asked Mara, giving a start. She often did when taken by surprise.

'Nothing's wrong.' Fiona gave her a complaisant smile. 'Something wonderful's happening – I'm getting the vibrations! I looked in the crystal ball just now and I saw it – I saw your slide. A lovely slide with a red butterfly on it; that's the one, isn't it?'

Mara shrank back a little, but Tish was already up on her feet, delighted by this interesting turn of events. It had been boring today. Nothing exciting had happened!

'Where was it?' she grinned. 'Did you see, Fiona?'

'I need Mara to come with me,' said Fiona importantly. 'She *must* be present. I need her to touch the crystal ball!'

Mara shrank back still further. 'No!' she said. 'I don't want to. It's not a crystal ball anyway. It's just an old cracked bathroom light globe!'

'Oh, Mara, don't be a spoilsport!' exclaimed Elf.

They all crowded round Mara, dragging her to her feet. This was going to be fun!

'Come on, you've been looking for that slide for ages!'

'Fiona's getting the vibrations!'

Rebecca joined in, gripping Mara gently by the arm. She was wide awake now! 'Come on, Mara. Be a sport. Let's go and see what Fiona says! You don't have to go on your own. We'll all come with you.'

So they dragged Mara along the corridor to Fiona's room in a giggling, whispering throng – the three As coming out into the corridor to see what the excitement was about, tagging on to the end of the procession.

'You can't all get in!' said Fiona as they crammed into the room.

'It's all right, some of us can watch from the doorway,' said Anne Finch. 'Don't shut the door, Fiona!'

The room looked shadowy and mysterious, lit only by the dim reading light above Fiona's bed. The crystal ball gleamed dully on the bedside table. Fiona sat down on the edge of her bed, peering into the globe's depths, and signalled to Mara to come and sit beside her. Reluctantly, Mara did so, helped along by a push from her friends.

'Now – place your fingertips lightly on the side of the glass – here,' said Fiona, taking hold of Mara's wrist. 'That's right. Everyone – Sssh! I've got to concentrate *very* hard.'

There were a few moments of absolute silence while Fiona peered and frowned. Then:

'I can see it again!' she cried. 'Now I can see where it is!'

'Where?' whispered Mara, licking her dry lips.

'It's lying somewhere green. It seems to be stuck behind a green pipe – and there's a green wall. It's a tiled wall, I think. Green tiles, with sort of steam on them –'

'The bathroom!' shrieked Tish in excitement. 'That's got green tiles all round the walls!'

'And green water pipes, running along the bottom, under the wash-basin!' cried Elf.

The two of them led the stampede along the corridor towards the bathroom.

Rebecca followed more slowly, her arm round Mara's shoulders, because Mara had gone very pale.

And then Tish emerged from the bathroom waving the red butterfly hairslide –

'Look, Mara! Look! It must have fallen off the

sill when you were brushing your hair! It was down behind the pipes. Fiona got it right!'

Mara just burst into tears!

Fiona took a few lumbering steps towards her, towering over her.

'What's the matter? Aren't you pleased?'

Mara turned to face Fiona and then backed slowly away.

'Don't you come near me!' she screamed. 'Go away! Go away!'

She turned and fled to her own room, rushed in and slammed the door behind her!

At that moment Margaret Exton appeared from upstairs. She came rushing down in her dressing gown.

'What on earth's going on? It sounds like a herd of elephants running up and down the corridor. Doors slamming! If you don't shut up this minute I'll go and find Mrs Barry. Go to bed all of you! And *quietly!*'

The Fifth Year girl stood there looking ferocious, arms akimbo.

They all scattered.

When Rebecca and Co. tiptoed into their room, they found that Mara was already in bed.

'Mara?' whispered Tish anxiously. 'Don't you want your slide now it's been found?'

But Mara was hiding under the bedclothes, the covers pulled right up over her head, too scared to say a word.

# ELEVEN
## What the Sand Revealed

Rebecca flopped into bed herself after that and fell into a deep sleep. It had all been too much! Mara was very soon asleep anyway, which was probably for the best.

The others waited up for Sue. Mr Barrington, who was the school's Director of Music, brought her back in his car. Then the four of them conferred in whispers in Elf and Margot's room about what had happened, nervously munching their way through the entire contents of Elf's biscuit tin, till gone eleven.

'Look, this is getting ridiculous,' said Tish at one point. 'We'll have to do something about it.'

'But what?' asked Elf, helplessly.

'Fiona really must have second sight!' whispered

Margot, in amazement. 'I don't think I was really convinced before. But now I am. If she has, well she can't help having it, can she?'

The black girl made it sound like an eye infection.

'No, but *we* can't have Mara going round scared to death!' said Tish.

'Well, we could tell Fiona to stop it,' suggested Sue, yawning with tiredness.

'That wouldn't do any good now!' replied Tish. 'The damage is done.'

'Well, what can we do about it then?' asked Elf again.

'I don't know. We'll have to try and think of something!' said Tish.

They were at a loss.

Next morning, Rebecca was the last to wake up. She yawned and stretched, grateful that it was Sunday and she'd had the chance to sleep in. She felt better now!

She looked towards the next bed and saw that it was empty.

'Where's Mara?' she asked, sitting bolt upright in her pyjamas.

'Gone out,' said Tish, who was up and dressed. She was the only other person in the room. The others were downstairs cooking breakfast as they were allowed to at weekends. 'Oh, Rebecca, I feel so guilty!'

Tish came and sat on the end of Rebecca's bed; she was holding the red butterfly slide.

'Where's Mara gone then?' asked Rebecca.

'She says she's going to spend all morning at the Hilary, doing her piano practice! It's obvious she hates being in Court House now, with Fiona just along the corridor. She won't even look at her slide or touch it –' Tish held it out, to show Rebecca. 'She says it gives her the creeps!'

'Oh dear,' said Rebecca. Then she frowned. 'I don't think I believe in ESP,' she said.

'To be honest, I don't know whether I do or not,' confessed Tish. 'But I can't think how else Fiona does it. And it all seemed so exciting – really fascinating!'

'It did,' agreed Rebecca. 'It is!'

'But I'm worried about Mara,' said Tish, miserably. 'We should never have encouraged Mystic Meg last night – I'd no idea that Mara would be so terrified!'

'I think Mara's probably been frightened all along,' said Rebecca uneasily. 'That's why she didn't want to believe in it!' She was feeling guilty herself. 'We shouldn't have got carried away. But – honestly! Mara's been on about that slide for ages! And now it's been found. D'you think Mystic Meg might have *noticed* it'd slipped down behind the pipes and that's why she was so excited?'

'Possible,' said Tish.

'Tish, did you get the feeling that Fiona was really hoping that Mara would be pleased and would like her? The look on her face when Mara screamed at her like that! She looked so upset. She wanted to be friends.'

'Didn't work, did it?' said Tish, wryly.

'*That* is the understatement of the year!'

As soon as Sunday lunch was over, Tish, Sue and Rebecca cornered Fiona just as she was coming out of the dining hall. They'd been looking for her all morning without success. She always seemed to be going off lately, somewhere along the beach in her tracksuit.

Mara had been hiding over in the music school all morning and now she was planning to spend the afternoon in the library. 'I shall sleep in Court House, that is all!' she'd said to Margot at lunch time. 'I do not like living there any more.'

It was turning into an impossible situation.

'Look, Fiona, can you lay off the fortune-telling from now on?' asked Tish.

'Mara doesn't like it,' said Sue.

'I gathered that,' said Fiona, impassively. 'You needn't worry. I'm not going to use my powers to help people and then just be screamed at.'

Fiona had already come to a decision that morning. She was fed up with trying to make friends with the crowd in Court House – at least she'd found somewhere to go, something to do with her spare time now. But she hated not having any friends at school. Mara being scared like that – how embarrassing! She'd even run away and hidden in the bushes before lunch, just because she'd seen Fiona approaching. Otherwise they'd have met up on the footpath near the Hilary Camberwell. Scuttled away like a frightened rabbit! It hadn't escaped Fiona's notice.

'At least she won't go round saying those things about me now,' thought Fiona.

But what a price to pay!

It was already an impossible situation. Fiona thought so, too. And secretly she was beginning to feel very unhappy at Trebizon.

So it was lucky for all concerned that Robbie Anderson liked Rebecca Mason and had given her a silver brooch.

And it was an even greater stroke of luck that she'd lost it!

It was just after two o'clock when Rebecca discovered that she'd lost Robbie's brooch.

Laura had fixed a practice match for four o'clock, Tigers v Cubs. But right now Rebecca was relaxing on the bed upstairs, writing her Sunday letter to her parents and telling them all her news. She decided to tell them about the brooch and had a sudden impulse. She'd make a little drawing of it, to show them! She fished around in her locker to find it.

It wasn't there!

Rebecca straightened up from the locker, feeling alarmed. Her heartbeats were racing. She'd *thought* she must have taken it off her blazer when she came back to the room on Friday evening. That was because it was no longer pinned under the lapel the next day.

But supposing she hadn't taken it off? She couldn't remember doing so, after all! Supposing it had come unfastened and dropped off somewhere? That would have been on Friday!

Quickly she rammed the pad of airmail paper, with its unfinished letter, under her pillow – just as Sue came into the room. Her sandy-coloured hair was damp and springy after being washed and she was looking for her hair dryer.

'Anything wrong?'

'No, nothing,' said Rebecca quickly.

She left the room and walked slowly down the stairs, thinking hard.

Where had she been in the blazer on Friday? Could the brooch have dropped off in Mrs Barry's sitting-room? No – Mrs Barry would soon have found it and guessed who it belonged to.

The beach. That was the most likely place!

She ran all the way across the grounds, round the back of old school and down through the little spinney at the back of Juniper House. She let herself out of the small gate that led directly on to the dunes at the top of the beach.

She scrambled to the top of the nearest dune, the high one, where she and Tish had sat and watched the sunset. No sun today – just bright cloud and a chilly wind.

She fell to her knees and scrabbled around with her hands in the sand, anxiously searching. No sign of it. But the sand was so fine, the wind was blowing it about, even now. The brooch could easily have got covered up –

She located the exact spot where she'd sat. She dug carefully all around and then –

A sudden gleam of silver!

'Oh, hurray!' Rebecca cried out. She'd found it!

She stood up, cradling the brooch in the palm of her hand, gently dusting it clean with her handkerchief. All intact! She turned it over and tested out the clasp. It seemed to work perfectly. 'I couldn't have fastened it properly,' she thought. 'Oh, what luck. I don't deserve to be so lucky!'

With the toe of her shoe she kicked some sand back into the little holes she'd dug – she suddenly felt ridiculously happy!

Just for luck, she took a final flying kick at a pile of sand nearby – and then gasped.

Something had flown out of it. Whatever *was* it? It looked like . . .

She bent and picked it up and stared at it in amazement.

'What's this doing here?' she wondered. 'It doesn't make sense.'

Rebecca walked back to school very slowly, deep in thought, searching her memory and trying to piece together all the clues – and at last she realised that she had the answer. A great feeling of anger swept through her – and then she had to laugh – and then she felt angry again.

When she got back to the room she found Tish and Sue having a conference.

'The others are stuck with Mara in the library!' said Tish. 'I mean, nobody wants to leave her on her own all the time, brooding, and she *refuses* to come back here. Fiona's completely unnerved her. We're trying to think what to do.'

'The point is,' said Sue, frowning, 'has Fiona got second sight, or hasn't she?'

'She hasn't!' stated Rebecca.

The other two stared at her. 'What?'

'She's not a clairvoyant at all!' exclaimed Rebecca. 'And I'm going to prove it.'

And so a few minutes later, Tish, Margot and Elf dragged Mara back to Court House. Mara was very excited and only a tiny bit nervous.

Apparently Rebecca had found out how Fiona had done everything. She didn't have special powers at all. She was a complete fraud!

Rebecca wouldn't say how she knew – she was keeping it as a surprise. They were going to play a trick on Fiona. They were going to teach her a lesson! It must be all right, if Rebecca said so.

Even so, just outside Fiona's room, she hesitated. The door was partly open.

Rebecca and Sue had got the tall girl cornered in there. They'd made her get the crystal ball out again. She was getting it out from under the bed and looking flustered.

'It's all right, Mara,' Rebecca called. 'Come in!'

Mara saw that Rebecca's blue eyes were very determined-looking. Her own eyes began to shine with anticipation. This looked as though it were going to be exciting!

'Right,' said Rebecca. Sue had taken the crystal ball from Fiona's unwilling hands and plonked it on the bedside table. 'Now, come on, Fiona – sit down and look in the crystal ball. Elf, can you draw the curtains shut for us? We want a bit of atmosphere.'

Elf did so and Fiona sat down on the edge of her bed, beside the crystal ball, looking sullen and worried.

Mara's confidence began to increase.

'Look here,' said Fiona, 'this is a waste of time. It's all very well saying you're going to give me a test. But what's that supposed to prove? You ought to know a person can't just be clairvoyant to order. Supposing I don't get the vibrations –'

'You got them last night quickly enough,' said Sue.

'Shut up making excuses!' added Tish. 'The test Rebecca's going to give you is so *easy*. You ought to be able to do it in your sleep. A person of your capabilities!'

Fiona didn't like Tish's tone of voice at all. It was challenging, and it made her smart.

'All right then,' she said. 'Give me the test.'

'Everybody quiet!' said Rebecca.

She took out of her pocket the red butterfly slide that had been found in the bathroom.

'See this, Fiona? It's the slide, yes?'

Fiona nodded.

'Now I'm going to turn my back and put it in either my left hand or my right hand.'

Rebecca turned and faced the curtains and did so. Then she turned back to face them all with both fists tightly clenched.

'Now, it's in my hand – but *which* hand is it in?' She placed her clenched fists on each side of the glass globe. 'There, you should be able to feel the vibrations. Look into the crystal ball and tell me which hand I've got the slide in.'

Fiona swallowed hard.

'All right.' She stared deeply into the glass, at the same time glancing from one fist to the other. The room had gone very silent. Silent and shadowy.

Mara licked her lips nervously. Did Rebecca

know what she was doing? Supposing Fiona got it right? She might easily get it right! And then they couldn't be sure . . .

But Tish turned and gave Mara a huge wink, and the Greek girl relaxed.

'Come on, Fiona,' said Rebecca, softly urging her.

Fiona took a deep breath, closed her eyes, then opened them.

'LEFT!' she said.

Rebecca laughed.

'Wrong!' she cried. Slowly she opened her right hand and showed her the slide.

They all started to giggle.

'But I didn't really get any vibrations –' Fiona began to protest.

'Sssh!' said Tish. 'We've got to give Fiona a fair chance. We've got to let her try again, haven't we?'

'We'll keep on and on, until you get it right,' said Rebecca. 'What could be fairer than that?' She was still feeling very angry with Fiona.

She turned her back, fidgeted a moment, then turned round, both fists clenched again. Once more she placed them each side of the crystal ball.

'Okay. Which hand this time?'

Again Fiona appeared to concentrate.

'RIGHT!' she said.

'Wrong!' said Rebecca – and showed Fiona the slide in her left hand.

She kept on repeating the operation.

Every time Fiona got the wrong hand. Every single time! She was beginning to look very red-faced and foolish. If she said 'left', Rebecca would show her the slide in her right hand and if she said 'right', then Rebecca would show her the slide in her left hand. By this time Mara was beginning to get puzzled. But the air of suppressed hilarity in the room grew and grew until finally Fiona burst out desperately –

'Stop it!'

Tears were starting up into her eyes.

'You've got both the slides, haven't you!' she said miserably.

'Yes,' said Rebecca quietly. She opened both hands together for the first time. Mara gave a little gasp. There were two identical red butterfly slides. One in the palm of each hand. 'On my left, slide A. It belongs to Mara and I found it in the sand dunes this afternoon. On my right, slide B, which you bought from Woolworth's yesterday and then hid behind the pipes last night –'

As Fiona nodded her head miserably, Rebecca added softly:

'Just like you took Sue's rosin out of her violin case and hid it behind the radiator!'

Sue sniggered nervously at that. But Tish was staring at the kettle on Fiona's formica-topped table with a rather grim expression on her face.

'And the first slide is really mine –?' Mara was asking eagerly. 'Slide A?'

Rebecca handed it to her.

'Yours, Mara. Clasp well worn. The other one's brand new. I *thought* there was something odd about it! This one's yours all right.'

Mara examined it happily and then nodded.

'The sand dunes. Of course! I went for a walk and sat there one evening!'

Rebecca threw the worthless slide on to Fiona's bed while Mara fastened her own in her hair and smiled gratefully. 'That feels better. Oh, *thank* you, Rebecca!'

'Isn't it about time Fiona did some explaining herself now?' said Tish. She had found her voice at last. It was very cold. 'Come on, Fiona. What about the biggest triumph of all – Rebecca's computer rankings. Let's hear it in your own words!'

Fiona buried her face in her hands and her shoulders began to heave.

'Don't, Tish!' Rebecca said quickly. 'Don't make her say –'

'*Did* you telephone London?' asked Mara. Her voice was surprisingly sympathetic.

'Of course she didn't!' Tish pointed at something. 'When I first walked into the room I stared straight at the kettle. I was just thinking how nice it was to have your own kettle. Then I saw the look on Fiona's face. Talk about a guilty conscience!' She turned and glared at Fiona now. 'You pinched Rebecca's private letter, didn't you? You must have pinched it from the mail board *on the Friday morning*! Tell us what you did then –'

'The kettle!' exclaimed Sue, shocked. 'You steamed it open with the kettle!'

'And then sealed it up again and held on to it till the *Monday*!' cried Margot, outraged. 'And all the time you knew Rebecca was waiting for it –'

'Please stop it!' begged Fiona. She looked them all in the eye now. The tears were streaming down her cheeks. 'I'm so ashamed. I'd give anything in the world not to have done it. It was that which made everything get out of hand! Once I'd done that, I could never explain, I could never go back –'

'It's all right, Fiona,' Rebecca cut in. 'You don't have to say any more.'

She'd guessed the truth earlier. She'd worked it out for herself. It was such an incredible thing to do – such an incredible cheek! – that it was the one explanation that had never occurred to any of them. But once Rebecca knew for certain that Fiona was a fraud, and had been prepared to go to such lengths to shut Mara up, it figured that she must have something pretty bad to hide. That was how Rebecca had worked her way back to the answer – and been angry enough to want to teach Fiona a lesson.

But she wasn't angry now.

And Mara humbled them all. She went across and put her arms round the crying girl.

'Don't cry, Fiona! Not when I am feeling so happy! You are nice! You are just an ordinary person after all! That makes us feel wonderful!'

The big girl blinked in surprise as Mara got out a handkerchief and wiped the tears off her cheeks. 'You mustn't cry; Court House is a happy place to be!'

'But you're all so good at everything!' said Fiona. She was starting to feel better already. She could talk to them now. 'Almost the first thing I heard someone say was that Rebecca might win Wimbledon one day. It made me feel so inferior! I just felt I had to do something really *clever* and try to make an impact. The most dramatic thing I could think of. And then Elizabeth's party was coming up and I was planning just to play that trick with Sue's rosin. But then I saw Rebecca's letter on the mail board on the Friday morning. It had just arrived – no one else was back from breakfast! It was spur of the moment . . .' She paused, ashamed. 'Once, at my last school, I did a fortune-telling act and guessed something right and I was popular for weeks!'

They all felt sorry for her now.

Rebecca swallowed hard. Her first term at Trebizon came vividly back to mind. How lost she'd felt! It had been awful, arriving in the Second Year. Everybody else seemed to have friends already – nobody seemed to notice you. She'd wanted to make her mark in some way, too!

'Cheer up, Fiona,' she said. She took hold of her arm and pulled her up. 'Let's go along to the Common Room. We'll make you a cup of coffee.'

They steered her towards the door, the centre of a protective throng.

Suddenly Tish broke away and went back into the room and picked up the old bathroom globe.

'What are you going to do with that?' asked Fiona, as they walked along the corridor.

Tish grinned.

'The dustmen collect the rubbish tomorrow,' she said.

They were all drinking coffee together in the little Fourth Year Common Room when Mrs Barrington marched in.

The six had been getting on rather well with Fiona. Behind that implacable exterior she had quite a jolly sense of humour. It was surprising how quickly they were talking like conspirators. They all agreed that the best way of letting the fortune-telling business die a natural death was to put the story around that Fiona knew somebody in London who had something to do with the computer rankings, and that the rest had all been intended just as a bit of fun to liven up life at Trebizon.

'That bit's certainly true!' laughed Tish, back in her usual bouncing form. 'You certainly did liven things up around here. Even if you did go too far!'

And then the House Mistress tapped on the door and marched in.

She looked very stern.

'So there you are, Fiona! I want a serious talk with you. You know the town beach is out of bounds. I'm rather surprised to hear about your behaviour!'

The six friends glanced at each other uneasily. What was this all about? Whatever it was, it was none of their business, and it would be humiliating for Fiona to be told off in front of an audience. Hadn't she suffered quite enough in the way of humiliation for one day?

Tish scraped her chair back and was the first to her feet.

'We're just going, Mrs Barry.'

'There's no need!' said the House Mistress sharply. 'It concerns you, too. All of you!'

# *TWELVE*
## Miss Willis Makes a Suggestion

'What's wrong with the sports programme we have in school?' asked Mrs Barrington, cross with Fiona's behaviour. 'There are umpteen things to do here – but apparently they're not good enough for you. The prefects tell me you've been going elsewhere for recreation. To the town beach, in fact. Meeting boys – messing around playing football! Not just once, either; they say you've been making a habit of it!'

Fiona went red to the roots of her hair. Rebecca felt sorry for her.

'Football!' said Tish, leaning forward and gazing at Fiona with interest.

'Look,' said Rebecca, starting to sidle towards the door. 'This isn't any of our business, Mrs Barry. Surely we can go now?'

It was embarrassing – Fiona getting a dressing down in public! And Elf was so nervous, she was going to giggle at any moment – Rebecca could recognise the signs, the bulging cheeks, the pretending to blow the nose. That would be the last straw!

'Not messing around – they let me play with them,' Fiona was mumbling indignantly. 'They train every day – they're top of the Wessex Youth League.'

Elf hiccuped but Tish was looking intent and saying 'You haven't been playing with the Colts, have you?' just as Mrs Barry clapped Rebecca on the shoulder with an iron hand and rasped:

'Come back here and sit down! What do you mean, this isn't any of your business?'

Rebecca scuttled back to her chair. The House Mistress surveyed them with a stony gaze, her arms folded. Elf's desire to giggle suddenly evaporated.

'It's everyone's business, and especially all of yours!' said Mrs Barry quietly.

She looked at Fiona and then at each one of them in turn.

'D'you know, I've been searching for Fiona and this was the very last place I expected to find her?' she said drily. 'In her room, alone, yes. Or over at Juniper House, trying to make friends with the juniors, perhaps. But in here – having a coffee with you lot, that makes a nice change, I must say.'

They all began to wriggle uncomfortably in their chairs – all except Tish, who was sitting stock still and staring at Fiona, bursting to speak. Rebecca was thinking guiltily that she'd mainly seen the new girl only at lesson times – what with tennis and hockey and having fun with her friends and trying to catch up with coursework in the library in the evenings! But even so, you could always make time if you really wanted to . . .

Mara was beginning to look quite tearful with remorse.

'The fact is,' Mrs Barry was saying, 'that nobody's made much effort to look after Fiona while she settles in here. All wrapped up in your own affairs! You six girls have got so much to give – but you seem to be getting thoroughly cliquey,' she added scoldingly. 'It's hardly surprising, in the circumstances, that Fiona's been finding her own diversions – pretending to tell the juniors their fortunes – oh yes, I know all about that. So you needn't look surprised – and now playing football with a crowd of small boys!'

Apart from Tish, the six friends looked shamefaced. Of course Mrs Barry didn't know about all the complications, but even so there was still some truth in what she said. Rebecca felt it keenly.

But suddenly Tish laughed – laughed out loud! And Fiona seemed to be in on the joke.

'Oh, Mrs Barry, they wouldn't be very pleased to hear themselves described as a crowd of small boys! Not the team that's top of the Youth League –'

'What team's that?' asked the House Mistress, frowning.

'The Trebizon Colts!' exclaimed Tish. 'That's right, isn't it, Fiona?' Fiona nodded as Tish continued: 'They're strapping – about six foot tall!'

'How do you know that?' asked Sue in surprise.

'I've seen pictures of them in the local paper,' said Tish. 'Your dear brother goes to watch them play. Don't you ever talk to your own brother? You know what a soccer fanatic Edward is! He's furious they don't play it at Garth. But Fiona – how on earth?' – it was the question Tish had been bursting to ask – 'I mean, *those* boys take their football seriously! D'you mean to say when they train they don't *mind* you joining in –?'

'Not in the least,' said Fiona. 'We practise tackling, passing – that sort of thing.'

They were all agog now. Even Mrs Barry was taking a sudden interest.

'You can hold your own with them, then?' asked Tish.

'Well, I'm big enough,' said Fiona, with a wry smile. Then, shyly, she added: 'As a matter of fact I play for a women's soccer team back home. The Burton Bluebells. Actually, *we're* top of *our* league too –'

The friends exchanged looks of amazement. A women's team? Top of their league? This was truly impressive.

'Fiona!' shouted Tish in excitement. The others were still trying to come to terms with this revelation. But Tish was already several jumps ahead. 'WE NEED YOU!'

And then Laura burst into the room.

'Are you coming, or aren't you? We're all waiting – ooh, sorry, Mrs Barry.'

'Laura! Laura!' Tish was on her feet, pulling Fiona to hers. 'Fiona plays football – she's really good. *Please* say you'll give her a trial for the Tigers now! – This minute! I think she's the person we're looking for.'

'I'm no good at hockey, I've tried it,' protested Fiona, trying to pull back. 'The ball's too small, I miss it with the stick! I keep wanting to kick it and you're not allowed to.'

'Somebody is!' laughed Tish.

'Kicking full-back!' said Laura. She was as excited as Tish now. 'Oh, yes – come on, Fiona. Let's give you a try. If you're no good, we'll soon say so.'

They all pulled Fiona to her feet and enthusiastically started to push her from the room.

'May we go now, Mrs Barry?' Rebecca called back, as an afterthought.

'Of course,' she said. She was smiling.

As they disappeared noisily into the corridor she gave a satisfied nod. 'That's better. That's more like it!' Humming to herself, she swiftly cleared away the coffee cups. 'I just hope Fiona lives up to their expectations.'

Mrs Barrington needn't have worried. Tish's hunch was right. Fiona Freeman, playing in the kicking full-back position in the Tigers' team in place of a goalkeeper, was really formidable!

Rebecca was playing for the Cubs, in their forward line-up. She soon discovered what it was like to have a face-to-face confrontation with Fiona – to find her looming up large in all her towering bulk, deftly kicking the ball clean off your stick, then rampaging on down the field with the ball in her own possession. It was an awesome experience! In spite of her size, she moved fast, she tackled fearlessly and she could kick the ball clear – down to her half like a bullet from a gun. The Tigers piled up goal upon goal!

'Poor Jenny!' thought Rebecca, catching a glimpse of their regular goalkeeper's face at one stage.

Jenny was standing on the sidelines watching the game. She looked utterly crestfallen.

All that changed after half-time.

Laura and Miss Jacobs conferred. Fiona had come through her trial in the back position with flying colours – but how versatile was she? Would she be equally good in goal? She was strong and aggressive and knew how to pile on pressure, but what would she be like restricted to goal and put under pressure herself?

They asked Fiona to put on the goalie pads and take over as goalkeeper for the Cubs, and they brought Jenny back into goal for the Tigers.

Sue, Eleanor and Wanda – and then for a time Rebecca – as the Tigers' leading strikers battered relentlessly at the Cubs' goal, and Fiona let through five goals. The game ended with three penalty strokes going straight home as well. When the Cubs played off their two penalty strokes, Jenny made two brilliant saves and neither went home.

Fiona was no goalkeeper.

Jenny was much better.

'I think the solution's quite simple,' said Laura afterwards, gathering the Tigers round her. 'We offer Fiona a place in the squad as a sub. But Jenny stays in the team as keeper. On the day of the tournament we play Jenny against the tough sides, but substitute Fiona against the weaker sides.'

'Marvellous!' everybody agreed, although Miss Jacobs looked slightly worried about something.

Rebecca was delighted.

'Oh, Jenny I'm so pleased it's worked out like this,' she whispered.

'So am I!' said Jenny, with feeling. She looked extremely happy, as though a great weight had been lifted from her mind. 'To be honest, ever since I saw the Cats that day and watched that Beth woman in action, I've felt lacking! But now what *I* lack, Fiona's going to be able to make up.'

Fiona had been taking her pads off behind the goal and waiting nervously for a decision.

When Laura marched over to her and invited her to be a member of the Tigers squad, as a substitute, her large placid face became suffused with pleasure. 'Oh, was I really all right?' she said.

Rebecca, with the others, ran up and clapped her on the back.

'Congratulations, Fiona! You're so gentle off the field – and so intimidating when you're on it!'

'I bet Joss will be pleased when she hears we've

found you!' said Laura. 'But you'll have to practise stickwork, Fiona.'

'Wait till you see the strip we're going to wear!' added Jenny.

It was getting dark now, nearly tea time, and the two of them walked back to Court House together, deep in conversation.

The following Tuesday lunch hour, Miss Willis called Laura and Tish into her office at the sports centre. It was just after one of the regular work-outs in the gym and the rest of the squad had gone on ahead to get back to lessons.

'Look, about your tournament at Easter,' said the head of the games staff. 'There's going to be a slight problem. Fiona's a marvellous find, of course. Miss Jacobs has told me all about it. But we thought we'd better check the rules. I've just rung the organisers and it's as I thought –'

'What's wrong?' asked Tish quickly.

'You can't take *four* substitutes. Three's the maximum. Apart from anything else, they haven't the accommodation and we're taking the twelve-seater, so we wouldn't have a spare seat. But in any case, it's not allowed! That's definite.'

'Oh,' said Laura. She and Tish exchanged unhappy glances. 'But we *can't* drop Fiona.'

'Definitely not,' agreed Tish. 'But we *will* have to drop somebody then?'

'One of the other subs. Sheila . . . or Wanda . . .' said Laura slowly. 'Or . . . Rebecca.'

'They're all equally important,' wailed Tish. 'What an impossible decision!'

'May I make a suggestion?' said Miss Willis, kindly. 'Decide nothing – yet. In fact, say nothing about this – to anybody. It would be demoralising for those three to know that one of them is going to be dropped. Let them all remain in the squad and see how they shape up. Then Laura can make her decision much nearer the time. These difficult decisions usually resolve themselves, you know.'

So Tish and Laura agreed with Sara Willis's suggestion. What else could they do?

# _THIRTEEN_
## Rebecca's Horrible Week

February was a happy, busy month for Rebecca –
she'd never known the days so full! Somehow she
crammed it all in – practising for the seven-a-sides,
the physical fitness programme, all her school
work. And the tennis! Coaching at school with
Miss Darling, county coaching with Mrs Ericson,
daily games with Trisha Martyn or the redoubtable
Mrs Doubleday who drove up from the town to
play with her – and two Under-16 fixtures against
other counties. She did well in those and reasonably
well in the two competitions that Mrs Ericson had
entered her for.

'Everything hinges on Bristol at half-term now,'
the county coach told her. 'Your points are building
up and you'll have the chance to play Rita Sullivan

there, and hopefully Rachel Cathcart as well. If you beat both of *them*, then I don't see how you can fail to be accepted for the Prudential. Not now you've beaten Deborah Bond. Your first national tournament, Rebecca! What a landmark that would be!'

Rebecca didn't need telling. What a landmark, indeed. 'And what a surprise for Joss,' thought Rebecca.

Some nice things happened in February.

Fiona and Jenny and Elizabeth became great friends and started to go around in a threesome. Mara and Fiona got on well, too, discovering that they both liked the same kind of music. Sometimes they listened to cassettes together on Mara's machine – Fiona didn't have one – in the single room. Fiona came in for some criticism from the girls in Norris House, over not having the gift of second sight after all – and Mara was the first to come to her defence. She told Debbie Rickard and Co. that they had no sense of humour. Within a fortnight the whole thing was forgotten, especially now that Fiona was making a name for herself in a different way! A little knot of juniors, led by Sarah Butters, sometimes came and cheered from the sidelines whenever the big girl played in the sevens practices.

It was a great month for Tish Anderson.

She got into the First hockey Eleven, and she was not yet fifteen.

Laura was the first to congratulate her – Laura was like that – and Tish's five friends took her to Fenners in the town and bought her chocolate eclairs and Coca Cola.

*The Trebizon Journal* was published, with Rebecca's piece in it. She arranged for one copy to be sent to her parents, and another to her grandmother.

Then, just before half-term, the new strip arrived. The tops were a soft green colour, white stripes down the sleeves and the words TREBIZON TIGERS emblazoned across the front, exactly as Joss's mother had designed them. They came in an assortment of sizes but even the very largest was short in the arms for Fiona – however, she just laughed and didn't care.

'Don't we look professional!' she exclaimed, as they all pranced in and out of each other's rooms in the new tops. 'Oh, Rebecca – green suits you. It makes your hair look even more blonde.'

Rebecca surveyed herself in the mirror and smiled. It made her feel good to look good! And she *did* like the name 'Tigers'. She was filled with pleasurable anticipation.

'I *am* looking forward to going to Queensbury,' she said.

'So am I!' said Sue.

So was Rebecca's gran.

*Of course I understand, Becky dear!* she wrote back, when Rebecca had explained that she wouldn't be with her at half-term. *I'll be thinking of you in Bristol. And I'll look forward to the Easter holidays all the more. That's when you come up to play in that hockey tournament and I shall meet some of your friends at last. Will Robbie be coming up to watch by any chance?*

Robbie!

Rebecca still hadn't heard from him. She no longer even *half* expected to. Why should he have to chase after her! That wasn't the arrangement, was it? She'd telephone him once his exams were over, as she'd promised. She had it all planned.

And as it was his birthday over half-term, she'd send him a card.

She couldn't possibly ignore his birthday, could she?

He was staying on at Garth over half-term, apparently, not going home. There was a big rugby match on and anyway he wanted to do some swotting.

'He'll be seventeen, won't he?' said Tish. She looked humorous.

'I suppose he will,' said Rebecca, carelessly.

She wondered why Tish had bothered to say it. Maybe it had just been something to say. After all, it was an awkward situation in a way – Tish being his sister. She'd like to have discussed things, but she couldn't.

Trebizon broke up for half-term on the Friday. In the morning Rebecca posted the birthday card to Robbie at the Garth College address. After lunch she waved off all her friends and wished them happy holiday and they all wished her luck in return. She spent the afternoon playing singles against Mrs Doubleday on the staff court and after tea Mrs Barrington drove her to Bath, quite a long journey, and dropped her off at her Great Aunt Ivy's house. This had been arranged in advance.

'Have a good night's sleep – I'll pick you up at nine,' she said when she left them.

'Thanks, Mrs Barrington.'

The House Mistress was staying with friends in the centre of Bath, quite close to the famous Pump Room. She'd be picking Rebecca up each morning to run her into Bristol for the tournament. It lasted three days in all. Rebecca's relatives in England tended to be few in number, elderly, rather hard up and non-drivers. Great Aunt Ivy was no exception. But at least Rebecca wasn't tempted to stay up late. The old lady always went to bed shortly after nine o'clock.

It was an exhilarating tournament. Rebecca was at a peak of physical fitness – she had the hockey training to thank for that. She got as far as the quarter finals, beating one of her arch rivals in the computer rankings soundly on the way – Rita Sullivan. Unfortunately Rachel Cathcart got knocked out before Rebecca could play her – by the current British Under-16 number one, who in turn defeated Rebecca in the quarter finals 6–0, 6–3. All in all, a very respectable tournament. Rebecca had managed to stretch the number one in the second set, and there'd been some long and exciting rallies. She was glad she'd worn Robbie's brooch.

'She's the best player I've ever played against, apart from Joss Vining,' Rebecca said to Mrs Barry as they drove back to Trebizon on the Monday evening.

'Ah, yes, well she and Joss have always been great rivals,' said the House Mistress. 'Since they were eleven or so. They're almost exactly the same age. It'll be interesting to see what difference Josselyn's year in the States has made.'

Once again Rebecca wished she could have played against Joss at Little Manor that time. She looked forward to the day when she'd be able to do so. 'Until I've played against Joss again, I can't be sure of anything,' she thought. Most competitive people have a yardstick, and this was Rebecca's.

Because surely Joss would be a world class junior by the time she got back from the States?

Rebecca slept in late on Tuesday morning at Court House and then went to find Miss Darling, who helped her to fill in her entry forms for the Prudential. She had to give her most recent computer ranking and all her best results since. The tournament wasn't until after Easter but the deadline for application was Friday.

'And you'll have nothing more to add now, Rebecca. Not before Friday! So you may as well get it sent off.'

When Mrs Ericson phoned at the end of the morning to hear about Bristol, Rebecca said:

'Do you think I'll be accepted?'

'I'd feel happier if you'd had the chance to defeat Rachel Cathcart! It's not conclusive. All you can do now is post your entry and forget about it, Rebecca! Let's wait and see, shall we?'

Rebecca nodded.

The Barringtons gave her lunch in their private quarters. Court House seemed lonely and echoing, with everybody away on half-term. But they'd all be back this evening.

In the afternoon Rebecca wrote a long-overdue history essay about Elizabeth I. When she'd finished it, up in the room, she suddenly felt completely engulfed by the emptiness and silence of the building. Oh, it would be so nice to see Robbie again!

She ran downstairs to the phone, picked up the receiver, and then abruptly replaced it.

No! He was studying.

Besides, she wasn't going to run after him.

She'd told him she'd phone him after his exams. According to Laura, whose boyfriend Justin was in the same form as Robbie, that would be in two and a half weeks' time.

That would be soon enough.

But when Rebecca phoned Robbie in the middle of March, he appeared off-hand towards her.

He'd done well in his exams and he seemed pleased about that. But instead of suggesting that they meet each other in the town and have a coffee, as Rebecca had been secretly hoping, Robbie said:

'Look, Rebeck, I won't bore you with the details, but I'm rather busy with something at the moment. I'll be over to see you before the end of term. That's a promise.'

'Well . . . thanks, Robbie,' said Rebecca. Then quickly: 'Bye, then.'

The end of term. That was almost a month away!

It looked suspiciously like the cold shoulder.

And when, a few days later, Rebecca caught a glimpse of him in the front passenger seat of Virginia Slade's brand new blue car, cruising up Trebizon High Street, she went rigid. Virginia was the daughter of Robbie's House Master. She was in the Lower Sixth at Trebizon and had a driving licence now. She was driving the car and Robbie was sitting beside her and smiling and talking animatedly to her as the vehicle sailed along. Rebecca shrank back into a shop doorway so they wouldn't notice her.

'He's seeing Virginia again!' she thought in amazement. 'So that's it!'

Robbie had been very keen on Virginia once. But Rebecca thought it had finished long ago.

She found the sight of them together like that quite shattering somehow.

But even worse than that was the fact that, over the next day or two, Tish and Sue became distinctly odd with her. They didn't laugh and joke as much as usual. They seemed ill at ease.

On the Sunday afternoon she came into the room unexpectedly and caught them whispering. They fell silent and looked embarrassed. It was horrible! It had been a horrible week.

'They know about Robbie and Virginia,' thought Rebecca. 'They think I don't know!'

But she just couldn't bring herself to say anything.

And all that week, of course, she'd been waiting on tenterhooks to hear if she'd been accepted for the championship. According to Mrs Ericson, the first acceptances had already come through – so obviously Rebecca was a borderline case. She began to feel very dubious about her chances. She remembered Joss's crushing words with a new sharpness and clarity. It was all part of feeling low-spirited.

The reason that Tish and Sue felt awkward with Rebecca had nothing to do with Robbie.

She was quite wrong about that.

It was because they knew that Laura had now come to a decision, and was going to have to break the news very soon. As Miss Willis had foreseen, these things often had a way of resolving themselves. It was now becoming clear who should be dropped from the squad. While Rebecca had been concentrating hard on her tennis, the other two – Wanda and Sheila – had been getting regular matches with the school's Third Eleven. On top of that they'd been to all the sevens practices, some of which Rebecca had now missed. They definitely had the edge.

'I'm sorry, Rebecca, it's awful,' said Laura. She'd left it till the Sunday evening. She was quite tearful about it. 'But those are the rules.'

For Rebecca, it was a fitting end to a horrible week.

# FOURTEEN
## Secret!

After Laura left Court House on the Sunday evening, Rebecca went upstairs with leaden footsteps and found Fiona Freeman waiting for her at the top of the stairs.

'I offered to drop out of the squad, Rebecca!' said Fiona. She looked distressed. 'I begged and begged Laura to let me stand down. She wouldn't let me.'

'I should think not!' said Rebecca indignantly.

But she was very touched. And for Fiona's sake she said quickly:

'You don't know what a relief it is! I've got far too much on at the moment. It's all turned out for the best.'

'Really?' said Fiona. 'Oh, Rebecca, do you really mean that?'

Rebecca turned away, hardly able to get the words out.

'Yes – yes, it's fine. Honestly!' So saying, she signalled goodbye and rushed off to her room. To her relief the other three seemed to have gone out. She shut the door behind her, threw herself face downwards on the bed and began to cry. Not just about the tournament but about other things as well – and most of all about Robbie.

Within moments Margot and Elf, who were in the interconnecting room without Rebecca having realised it, catching up on some GCSE coursework, both appeared at the bedside with anxious faces.

'Oh, now you've caught me being a baby!' wailed Rebecca.

Elf bit her lip worriedly.

'Oh, Rebecca, you mustn't be miserable! You've still got the tennis. Just think, you'll be playing in the Prudential, you'll have more time to practise!'

'They haven't accepted me!' hiccupped Rebecca. 'I'm *sure* I'm not going to be accepted. They haven't written! Besides, it's Gran I feel so awful about. She's really been looking forward to it –'

They let Rebecca snuffle into the pillow for a bit while they went and made her some cocoa. When they came back she was sitting up with her back propped against the pillows, her cheeks still rather tearstained.

'Can't you bring your gran over to watch the sevens anyway?' asked Margot helpfully.

'How can I?' asked Rebecca in despair. 'There aren't any buses.' She blew her nose. 'I was going to ask Miss Willis if she could go over once we got there – and pick her up in the minibus. I'm sure she wouldn't have minded, seeing I was going to be in the tournie!'

'Couldn't you and your gran go there together in a taxi?' suggested Elf.

'Gran would think that was pretty extravagant,' said Rebecca. 'I mean – with me not even playing. It just wouldn't be the same for her, would it?'

'No, it wouldn't be the same,' agreed Margot. She and Elf exchanged glances, while Rebecca drank her cocoa in silence.

'That was nice!' she said, draining her cup. She gazed round the room and asked suddenly: 'Where have the others gone?'

'Oh, just over to Garth to have coffee with Robbie and David and Edward,' said Margot, as casually as she could. 'Must be missing their brothers or something!'

Even as she said it, she realised how unlikely that sounded!

'I see,' said Rebecca. She placed the empty cup on her bedside locker, then raised her eyebrows. 'And Mara? She's gone as well?'

Rebecca could sense their embarrassment. It suddenly became crystal clear to her that there was some sort of fun occasion going on, involving Robbie, to which she'd not been invited.

'They haven't cycled there?' she asked curiously.

'I mean, it's dark. Whose car have they gone in?'

'They went off in – er – a blue one,' said Margot.

Virginia Slade's, presumably!

'I think I'll have a bath and go to bed,' said Rebecca. 'I'm tired.'

She was now more convinced than ever that Robbie and Virginia were going out together again, and that Tish and Sue knew about it and had been trying to keep it secret from her. That was why they'd been so funny towards her lately!

She went to bed very early indeed, and when the other three got back she was fast asleep.

But there was something different about Monday morning – a much happier atmosphere.

Rebecca sensed it from the moment she woke up. Was it the fact that Sue had drawn all the curtains back and the sun was streaming in? Or was it just the fact that it was the start of a completely new week and the Horrible Week was now behind her?

'Wake up, Rebecca!'

'We've made you a cup of tea!'

'It's a lovely morning!'

Suddenly Rebecca realised that her best friends were once again their normal selves – Tish cheerful and full of bounce, Sue quietly humorous – neither of them keeping her at arm's length any more!

'Here you are,' said Tish, 'tea in bed – *and* a biscuit. We're going to spoil you this morning. Oh, Rebecca, isn't it the most disgusting rule you've ever heard of that we can't have four subs in the squad?'

'Well, yes – I suppose it is,' said Rebecca, in surprise. For the first time since Laura had broken the news to her, she smiled. 'The most disgusting thing I've ever been told!'

'If you knew what we've *been* through,' said Sue. 'Having to keep the whole wretched thing secret from you!'

'It was agonising for Laura! She was the one who had to take the decision!' said Tish. 'Miss Willis swore us to secrecy ages ago, about the rules. She said to wait and see how things shaped up. But just these last few days, since I've guessed for sure what Laura's decision was going to be – and honestly, I think it's the right one, Rebeck – the strain has been *unbearable.*'

'I guessed something was going on,' said Rebecca. 'I just didn't know what!'

She felt an overwhelming sense of relief. Whatever the relationship between Robbie and

Virginia might or might not be, her friends were obviously not aware of it. Perhaps there was nothing going on, after all! That wasn't why they'd been embarrassed and secretive. It was to do with the sevens tournament – and Rebecca suddenly saw clearly what a strain it must have been for them.

She drank her cup of tea. She tried very hard to be philosophical.

'Miss Willis said I was trying to have my cake and eat it,' she said. 'I guess she was right.'

'You're going to be a tennis champion!' said Mara, coming in from the bathroom, still brushing her dark hair. '*That* is what you're going to be! Oh, Rebecca, it's such a lovely morning. Surely the postman will bring something today.'

Perhaps he would! Suddenly Rebecca felt optimistic even about that.

She climbed out of bed and went to get washed and dressed. When she returned in her school uniform, she said to Tish:

'To be honest, I know it's right – I'm not quite as good as the rest of you. It's just that Gran's going to be so disappointed.' Rebecca bit her lip. 'I should never have promised her.'

Tish had been staring out of the window

thoughtfully – but now whirled round to face Rebecca. She blurted out, all in a rush –

'Rebeck, it's an important day for Robbie today! I can't explain. But will you keep your fingers crossed for him?'

Rebecca stared at her in surprise. What *was* she talking about?

At once she was reminded of the fact that they'd gone somewhere last night and she hadn't been invited. Though Virginia Slade apparently had been. It was all very well for her to try and look on the bright side. But really . . .

'Why should it concern me if it's an important day for Robbie?' she said, rather coolly. 'Anyway –'

'It might concern you quite a lot –' began Tish, trying to butt in.

'Anyway, why don't you ask Virginia Slade to keep her fingers crossed?' finished Rebecca. 'I'm sure Robbie would prefer that. I mean, he obviously likes her.'

There. She'd said it!

Tish stared at Rebecca. Then, surprisingly, she gave a short laugh.

'Oh, Rebeck. You don't know my brother,' she said. 'He's such a bad type! It's not *her* he likes, you know. Just her car –'

At that moment, Sue walked in.

'Shut up, Tish!' she said and hurled her washbag at her. 'You're talking too much!'

'*What* is going on?' asked Rebecca, feeling a funny little flutter of excitement.

'Secret!' they cried in unison, but they were laughing.

'Honestly!' said Tish, as the bell went for breakfast. 'It really *is* a secret, Rebeck, so you mustn't ask any more questions. Just keep your fingers crossed, that's all.'

Whatever the secret was, Rebecca now realised – from the excited expressions on their faces – it was obviously a good one.

# FIFTEEN
## Magical Monday

Monday had started with the sunshine streaming in and it just got better and better. It was magical Monday as far as Rebecca was concerned.

When they all came back to Court House after breakfast the postman had been, and Mrs Barrington was so excited about the letter addressed to Rebecca that she gave it to her in person. 'Come on, open it! It looks like the one you've been waiting for!'

It was from the organisers of the tournament. At last!

And her entry had been accepted!

There were whoops of excitement in Court House and Mrs Barry at once phoned through to the Principal at her home in the grounds.

'Exciting news here, Madeleine,' she reported

happily. 'You may want to announce it at Assembly!'

Miss Welbeck did indeed tell the school at morning Assembly that Rebecca Mason of IV Alpha had been accepted for the Prudential after Easter, her first national tournament, and that the good wishes of the entire school went with her. For the rest of the day people kept coming up and congratulating her.

There was somebody else who wanted to congratulate her.

When she got back to Court House at the end of the afternoon, after a game of tennis with Trisha Martyn on the staff court, the rest of 'the six' were waiting for her out the front. Tish was dancing from one foot to the other in secret delight.

'Robbie's just phoned, you're to wait here!'

'He's coming over to see you!' exclaimed Mara, her brown eyes shining. 'He'll be here in ten minutes.'

The second tea bell went.

'What about tea –' said Rebecca, her heart going pit-pat.

'We'll save you some!' laughed Elf, giving Rebecca a push. 'Go and comb your hair or something.'

They all rushed off then towards the footpath

to old school and the dining hall, laughing and jostling one another and glancing back at Rebecca like a bunch of conspirators.

Rebecca shook her head, feeling slightly bemused.

Then she hurried upstairs, washed and tidied up, and came down again. She waited outside the front porch of the boarding house, leaning back against the glass and keeping a look out for the sudden appearance of Robbie on his bicycle. She felt nervous.

A red car drew up in the big gravelled forecourt – one that she'd never seen before.

It looked rather old, though newly painted, and its sunroof was open.

It parked sideways-on to Rebecca and she gazed across at it idly, wondering who the driver was, as the engine was switched off.

Suddenly she became aware that the person inside was standing on the seat and then –

A head and shoulders appeared through the open hatch in the roof. Thick dark curly hair, a boy's grinning face.

'Boo!'

'Robbie!' gasped Rebecca, in amazement.

She wanted to laugh as he ducked down inside again, opened the driver's door and climbed out. But she restrained herself. Instead she ran across to the car and scolded him.

'Robbie! You'll be in big trouble if you're caught.'

He'd always been car mad. He'd started learning to drive when he was only thirteen, on the Anderson family's bumpy paddock at home. Rebecca remembered the awful episode when he was accused of taking his House Master's expensive new car for a joy ride – Mr Slade had been furious with him. He'd been rusticated over that – until they'd found the real culprit. So what was he taking a chance like this for?

'Who's lent it to you?' Rebecca asked. 'Oh, Robbie, you're breaking the law.'

He drew himself up to his full height. He was trying hard not to laugh.

'What a rotten welcome! It's *my* car, and as from half an hour ago I'm allowed to drive it. I've just passed my driving test!'

'ROBBIE!' squealed Rebecca. Then – 'Are you joking or what? I thought you had to be incredibly old, about eighteen, or seventeen-and-a-half or . . .'

How dense she'd been!

Was seventeen the age at which you could get a driving licence then? It must be!

That's what Tish had been hinting at, when she'd sent Robbie his birthday card.

'Got it? Seventeen!' said Robbie, finishing her sentence. He looked elated. 'Incredibly old! That's me. Just call me Rip Van Winkle!'

'You've just taken your driving test? You've passed?' asked Rebecca, in wonder. '*Well.* Congratulations!'

'Congratulations yourself,' said Robbie. 'Tish

told me on the phone. About the Prudential. I just had to come over straight away. It's fantastic, Rebeck!'

Rebecca nodded. But she felt rather humble. She was walking slowly round the car now, touching it. A few things were slowly beginning to dawn on her, though not everything, not yet.

'This is really your car? Your own car? You bought it with your own money?'

Dr Anderson had told his son years ago that if he wanted to own a car one day then he'd better start saving up for it – and Robbie had taken him at his word. It was a standing joke in the family – Robbie's car fund – but Rebecca had secretly admired the way he'd always worked long hours on a local farm in the school holidays, religiously putting the money away in an investment account so that he couldn't touch it and it earned interest, too. But she'd never seriously thought he'd be able to save enough to buy a car all on his own, not for a long time yet, nor had she realised that the point at which he could get a driving licence was quite so imminent!

This was probably the most exciting day of his life and she'd never for a moment twigged what was going on, nor even thought about it very deeply. So wrapped up in her own affairs and her own futile emotions about Robbie and the fact that he hadn't come running the moment she'd phoned him that day!

'When did you get it, Robbie?'

'Over half-term. Mr Slade helped me find it. It was a real bargain, but it needed a lot of work done on it to get it through its MOT. I've been working on it every night since the end of exams. Murdoch's been helping me – so's Mr Slade. We had to strip the whole thing down.'

He patted the bodywork and beamed proudly.

'Right up to this weekend I was in a sweat about getting it through the test. But she's through now – and taxed and insured as well!'

'Did you celebrate last night, by any chance?' asked Rebecca wryly.

'Yes.' Robbie smiled awkwardly. 'It was Murdoch's idea. He's really helped me a lot, you know.' He was talking about Edward, the elder of Sue's two brothers, who was in his form at Garth College. David was a year younger and not as knowledgeable about cars as Edward. 'Of course, Murdoch is demanding use of the car when he manages to get a driving licence himself, but we'll have to see about that. Anyway, the fool went and asked Tish over – and Sue and Mara wanted to come as well! He got Virginia to drive them over – she's been giving me some practice, driving in traffic. Her father asked her to. But, anyway, I wasn't keen on celebrating the MOT – I was scared you'd find out.'

'Why didn't you want me to find out, Robbie?' asked Rebecca. She was reflecting that both Virginia and her father had reason to feel badly about the episode of the stolen car. They'd wanted to make it up to Robbie, perhaps.

'Well.' Robbie came closer to Rebecca and put his arm round her shoulders. He looked down into her face. 'Why d'you think? I wanted the whole thing to be a surprise for you. And I was in a sweat about my driving test. A car's no use if you haven't got a driving licence. And they're getting really strict now. Some of the boys say they fail you first time on principle! So how did I do?'

'Brilliantly!' laughed Rebecca. She felt very happy. She added in some amazement: 'And it was all so you could give *me* a surprise?'

'Of course!' he said.

Rebecca suddenly buried her face in his shoulder.

'Oh, Robbie – it was a lovely brooch – I have

missed you! That time I rang you – I thought you were fed up with me. I thought you were maybe saying goodbye.'

'Goodbye? Of course not! But it was awkward. You see, Tish told me you mightn't be going to your hockey thing – and you didn't know. And she knew how you were banking on it, and how you'd promised your grandmother, and so forth. She swore me to secrecy! I was dying to see you, but I knew that if I did I wouldn't be any good at hiding anything from you . . .'

'And so?' asked Rebecca. She'd gone very quiet.

'So I decided that if *only* I could get the car fixed in time *and* pass my test today – well, at least I could take you to watch the hockey thing. Your grandmother as well! I mean that'd be better than nothing –?'

'Oh, Robbie!' She looked up at him, but her eyes were misting over. 'Better than nothing? That's the best idea I ever heard. And Gran – she'd love to meet you!'

'D'you think she'll trust herself to my driving?' he asked solemnly.

'Well, if I can, she can!' said Rebecca, joyfully.

She knew she must go and join the others at tea

now. But before she left, Robbie took hold of her hand and pulled her back.

'Rebecca. Want to know something?'

'What, Robbie?'

'I've missed you, too.'

So that was Rebecca's magical Monday.

# SIXTEEN
## The Sevens – and What Joss Meant

Rebecca stirred sleepily. Where was she? She wasn't at school because the bed felt different. She opened one eye and saw the wallpaper with the flying geese on it. Of course – today was the great day and she was at Gran's! – in the little single bedroom there. Something had woken her up. It was the sound of the phone – its high-pitched warble piercing the silence of the small bungalow.

Then it stopped. Good. Robbie must have answered it. The phone was in the sitting room and he was sleeping in there on Gran's sofa.

Rebecca turned over and closed her eyes again. Just five more minutes . . .

Suddenly there was a crash followed by thumping

on the door.

'Rebeck! Wake up!'

That was Robbie's voice.

He pushed open the door and stood there, still in his sleeping bag, clutching it round his chest like a competitor in a sack race – then, legs trapped together in the bag, he took three bouncy little jumps across the room. His curly hair was tousled.

'Wake up!' he laughed, bending over and shaking her by the shoulder. 'Quick – you're wanted on the phone.'

'Uh?' Rebecca sat up in bed and looked at the clock, rubbing her eyes sleepily. 'It's only eight o'clock!' she protested. 'I'm still half asleep. If it's Tish, I'll kill her!'

'It isn't Tish,' said Robbie, bounding away in his sleeping bag. 'I'm in the middle of getting dressed! I'd better take my stuff to the bathroom.'

He disappeared into the hall. Rebecca got out of bed and stumbled to the door, tying up the belt of her dressing gown as she went. Across the hall the sitting-room door was open and her grandmother, who'd just started to cook breakfast, had come out of the kitchen to see what was happening and was hovering in the hall, looking flustered and excited.

'Hurry up, Becky!' she whispered. 'Who is it?'

'I don't know, Gran,' said Rebecca in bewilderment.

She scuttled into the sitting room. The phone was lying off its hook where Robbie had dropped it. She dived across to the telephone table and picked it up.

Today *was* the great day. It was Thursday tenth of April and the day of the girls' national hockey sevens at Queensbury Collegiate, the huge co-ed school situated in open countryside only a few miles from old Mrs Mason's home town.

They'd all broken up at Trebizon for Easter, the day before. The minibus had set off for Queensbury crammed full of girls, luggage and hockey sticks, every seat taken. Miss Willis and Miss Jacobs had planned all along to take the small bus, the twelve-seater, and when the time came to leave they'd found that Mara, Elf and Margot had plastered a huge sticker on the back – UP THE TIGERS! – and tied bunting and streamers to the rear bumper.

They decided to let these frivolities remain and there were loud cheers and cries of 'Good luck!' as the vehicle trundled off through the school grounds, followed slowly by a rather elderly red car with its sunroof open. Robbie's, of course, and he was driving, with Rebecca sitting beside him in the front passenger seat. The rear seats were full up with luggage.

'Yes, I *will* allow you to go home in Robbie Anderson's car,' Mrs Barry had told Rebecca when she'd asked permission. 'Your grandmother's agreed – and I gather from Mr Slade that Robbie's a very careful driver. But we all think it would be a sensible idea if you travel up in convoy with the minibus, as far as Queensbury. Besides, Miss Willis says she'd be most grateful if she could use Robbie's car as an overflow for luggage. They're going to be heavily laden.'

And so, bumping along the west country lanes and then all the way up the M5 into Gloucestershire, they had the back of the streamer-bedecked minibus in view. It was a cheerful sight. Rebecca felt very happy on that beautiful spring afternoon, leaning back in the passenger seat and letting the warm breeze which came down through the sunroof wash over her face as the countryside slid by . . . talking to Robbie, listening to music on the car radio, waving to Tish and Sue and the others when they looked back from time to time to see if they were okay behind.

Of course the underlying melancholy was still there, just the palest tinge, when she remembered that *she* wouldn't actually be taking part the next day. But this nearly made up for everything. And she'd been allowed to keep her strip – the beautiful green sweater with the white stripe. That had been important to her. 'Of *course* you must keep it, Rebecca,' Miss Willis had said. 'Browns have made up a top for Fiona which fits her properly, I'm glad to say. And in any case, you *are* a member of the Tigers and always will be, and it's only these wretched rules that make it impossible for you to play on the day. There may be another time! Besides –' she'd added with a laugh, 'your parents have already been docked for it, you know!'

They reached Queensbury Collegiate in the early evening, driving through wooded grounds awash with rivulets of swaying yellow daffodils, then past two meadows of grazing cattle (for the school farmed some of its two hundred acres) to the big modern buildings that housed over fifteen hundred students in term time. Most of them had dispersed on Monday.

Rebecca and Robbie only stayed long enough to hand over the luggage they'd brought up and then to join the others for a quick lemonade brought out to them from the school refectory. While they drank it, they all stood on a long veranda that overlooked a sea of green playing fields beyond. They gazed at hockey, soccer and rugby pitches – and watched some groundsmen putting the finishing touches to newly painted white lines on the nine hockey pitches. Ready for tomorrow's tournament. Laura and Joss ran down there to have a look.

'The pitches are hard as iron – very dry!' said Joss Vining, as she scrambled back up the steps of the veranda. 'Unless it rains tonight the ground's going to be really fast going!'

Like the rest of them she was at a peak of physical fitness, eager and strung up for the long-awaited seven-a-sides. The family had been back in England for over a week now and Joss had twice been across to Trebizon to practise with the squad. Rebecca had heard about this but on each occasion had been elsewhere, playing tennis. However, she'd sworn Tish and the others to secrecy about the Prudential.

'Don't tell Joss about it when you see her,' she'd said. 'I want to tell her myself. I'll choose the right moment.' Adding to Tish: 'I want to see the expression on her face.'

And Tish had smiled.

Wednesday evening had still not been the right moment. The veranda was crowded, some prefects from the host school were gathering up all the 'Tigers' to show them where to put their luggage – and besides, she and Robbie had to dash. Gran was expecting them.

'Bye, Rebecca –'

'Make sure you bring Biffy in the morning!'

'The first matches start at ten. Don't be a minute late!'

'I won't! D'you think I'd want to miss anything? Bye!'

Half an hour later they were sitting down together at Mrs Mason's dining-room table to a delicious meal of steak-and-kidney pudding, followed by trifle and whipped cream. It had been arranged in advance that Robbie would be put up on the sofa there for these two nights.

It had been a happy evening, Mrs Mason delighting in their company – so pleased to see Rebecca again and liking Robbie on sight. They'd made her laugh a lot and all three had stayed up late playing a good card game.

So Rebecca was still feeling very sleepy when she picked up the phone next morning.

'I'm sorry Rebecca, it's rather early. Have you got your strip with you?'

'Pardon?'

It was Miss Willis's voice!

'Has - has somebody left theirs behind?' she asked, with a shake in her voice.

'Worse than that, Rebecca. We want you to play. We need you back in the squad.'

'To play?' squeaked Rebecca, in disbelief.

Apparently Miss Jacobs had taken three of them out before breakfast - Wanda, Eleanor and Sue - to give them some last minute coaching. She'd practised giving them hit-ons and then - both diving for a ball at exactly the same moment - Wanda and Eleanor had crashed their heads together.

'What happened?' asked Rebecca. 'Are they badly hurt?'

'Wanda's got a huge bump on the head, but we're hoping she'll be fit by lunch time. Eleanor's come off worse. She was knocked out and she needs stitches. She can't possibly be allowed to play.'

'Oh, poor Eleanor!'

She'd trained so hard – she was such a fantastic little runner – what's more, the squad wouldn't be so good without her! And suddenly Rebecca realised something.

'But we're not allowed another sub, Miss Willis!'

'We haven't signed in yet,' the games teacher said urgently. 'That's why I've rung you up at once! We have to sign in by nine – an hour before play starts. Everyone signs by name and after that we're not allowed to make any changes. Can you hurry, Rebecca? Do you think you can make it?'

'Definitely!' exclaimed Rebecca. Her excitement was starting to mount. 'Nine o'clock? I'll be there, Miss Willis!'

What a rush!

They gobbled down their breakfast – Rebecca's grandmother was now so excited that she hardly touched her scrambled egg. Robbie finished it off for her. 'The washing up, I'll do the washing up!' she said. But Rebecca stopped her. 'No, Gran! *Leave* the washing up. Just go and get your handbag and a nice warm coat in case it gets chilly – and don't forget the front door key. I'll go and find my strip! Oh dear, I haven't got my hockey boots – or stick!'

'I'll go and make sure the car's going to start!' said Robbie with an anxious grin.

But they got there, and Rebecca signed in, with ten minutes to spare.

It was an incredible day, a day when stamina counted for all. The pitches were indeed like iron and the matches were played at a gruelling pace. The twenty schools in the tournament had been hand picked from all over the country – there were some brilliant players in evidence.

The teams were put into four groups of five – A, B, C and D. Before lunch they each had to play the other four teams in their group. The Tigers were in Group C. Rebecca played in all of these morning matches, which lasted fifteen minutes each way. A loud central klaxon signalled the start and finish of each contest – with no injury time or extra time for any reason allowed. Of course the other two substitutes, Fiona and Sheila, were both defence players. Wanda still looked very pale and needed the rest of the morning to recover, so Rebecca's presence in the forward line with Joss and Sue was vital.

Just before the first match started and they lined up on the pitch against the Skinnies, from

Skinnerton School in Dorset, Rebecca caught a flicker of uncertainty on Tish's face. It would be mainly up to Tish to check the Skinnies' legendary centre-forward, an amazingly tall girl who already played for the England 19 team. But Rebecca didn't think that was the reason for the uncertainty. She guessed that Tish must be thinking that at last her 'master plan' was to be put to the test.

It had been Tish's idea from the very beginning to put athletes as *well* as the best players in the squad today, because of the need for speed. She and Joss and Laura were both things. But once they'd got possession of the ball they needed sprinters like Aba or Eleanor – except now, once again, it was Rebecca – to burst about the pitch and be in the right place at the right time.

Tish needn't have worried. They got off to a good start.

It was a clever move of Laura's. She put in Fiona to reinforce Tish, so that the Skinnies' centre-forward found herself doubly checked by both a sweeper and a full back allowed to use stick, hands and feet, whenever she tried to break for goal. The Tigers held them to a 0–0 draw.

They won the other three matches in Group

C. Twice Rebecca scored on the rebound during a short corner – a move they'd rehearsed. By lunch time Tigers had qualified to play a cross-over against the crack Yorkshire Terriers, who were top of Group D, while the Skinnies played the runners-up in that group, a team from a school in London.

For the cross-over, after lunch, Laura substituted Wanda – now fully recovered – for Rebecca and the Tigers won 3–0, again from corners. Play was getting rough! As the Skinnies also won their cross-over they crossed-over yet again to play Queens from Group A in the semi-final, while the Tigers played Bluecoat Bears from Group B in their semi-final.

The Queens, who'd dreamt up the tournament in the first place and had hoped to win – they were tough and played mixed sevens sometimes with the Collegiate boys – suffered a shock defeat in their semi-final at the hands of the Skinnies. Aba, Laura, Tish and Joss on the other hand produced some of the most dazzling hockey of the afternoon – high whizzing passes taken from stick to stick on the run – to win their semi-final 4–1. Watching this match from the sidelines with Robbie and waving Biffy the bear for all she was worth, Rebecca nearly cheered herself hoarse. So did Miss Jacobs and Miss Willis!

Rebecca's gran had gone to have a cup of tea, and missed it.

So for the final it was Tigers v. Skinnies again.

When the klaxon sounded, Robbie rushed off to find Mrs Mason and then escorted her across the grass to the pristine pitch which had been saved up for the final, eager spectators gathered all round it.

Because Rebecca was back in the forward line! Borrowed hockey shoes, borrowed stick – but still very much needed!

Sue had been playing beautiful hockey all day, only this was match number seven and she was starting to get cramps. So Laura substituted Rebecca in Sue's place. She also decided to play Fiona again, as kicking full-back, in place of Jenny in goal.

But the Skinnies' centre-forward was wise to that now and just before half-time they scored a shock goal when she whipped the ball away from Tish with a reverse stick tackle, popped it straight between Fiona's legs as she charged – and it trickled into an empty goal.

It was half-time and the Tigers were 0–1 down.

They changed ends and Laura took out Fiona for Jenny, who'd been standing by in her goalie pads. The Skinnies were nearly exhausted now, but they pulled out a last big effort and battered at the Tigers' goal for the first minutes of the second half. Jenny made three great saves but missed the fourth. The Tigers were 0–2 down.

That galvanized them. Five minutes later Laura cleared from the edge of the circle with a beautiful long hit, taken by Tish who zigzagged down the field, passed to Rebecca who passed to Joss. Joss weaved her way round two defenders and imposed her authority with a magnificent goal that looked as though it would burst through the back of the net. She followed this up with a second goal three minutes later following a pass from Wanda taken from Aba on the run. The score was 2–2.

The spectators began to cheer loudly. There was a tremendous atmosphere.

Rebecca was tense. She knew that the Tigers had the edge now, they still looked fresh – and the Skinnies were starting to flag! But time was running out! She dreaded the harsh blast of the klaxon calling time. If that happened with the score 2–2, the victory would be decided on penalty strokes and might go to the Skinnies. They had some big hitters.

The Tigers *had* to score another goal – they must! Before it was too late.

The Skinnies were spinning out every second now – deliberately putting the ball out of play, to waste time, even though it meant a hit-on against them. They were banking on that klaxon sounding, as surely it must! Somebody started a slow handclap.

Joss took the hit-on. She stood behind the sideline, a spot of angry colour in each cheek, gave Rebecca a quick nod – then sped the ball across the turf towards her.

Rebecca picked the ball up cleanly on her stick and started to run like the wind.

Somehow she kept the ball on her stick ahead of her flying feet – racing towards the circle. She must score – she thought of Eleanor . . . she'd score a goal for Eleanor – she was in the circle now!

Out of the corner of her eye she saw a girl coming to tackle her, but she'd left it too late! Rebecca was going to score a goal! She lifted her stick high as she ran – to shoot –

Crash! She went flying!

She'd been tripped up. Quite deliberately.

The umpire's whistle went. Foul! Rebecca scrambled to her feet, the breath almost knocked out of her body, but she picked up her stick and glanced round.

The umpire was signalling a penalty flick.

Joss was running up to take it but Rebecca knew that there probably wasn't time. Then she heard a sharp little bleat from the whistle. The umpire was signalling to Rebecca to get on with it! The goalkeeper stood quite still . . .

The ball was at Rebecca's feet. She took a deep breath. She knew she was only allowed to move one foot. One, two, three . . . flick!

Rebecca's stick caught the ball clean and flicked it into goal, straight past the goalkeeper's left leg.

Then all three things happened at once – the blast of the umpire's whistle that said 'goal', the roar of the crowd – and the loud blare of the final klaxon.

It was all over!

Tigers had won 3–2.

'Rebecca!' they all squealed with delight, as they surrounded her on the pitch. Robbie rushed over and hugged her.

On the sidelines, Mrs Mason turned to a bystander and said proudly: 'That's my granddaughter, you know' – just as Rebecca looked her way and waved.

They all walked across then and Rebecca said –

'Come on, Gran. There's going to be a bit of a party! You can meet my friends properly now. There's Sue, just coming – and this is Tish.'

Tish grinned.

'How did we do, Mrs Mason?'

Then Tish caught Rebecca's eye and laughed with elation.

'Didn't I always say we'd win?'

It was a good party. It took place in the refectory,

after Laura had been presented with the huge silver trophy – Miss Willis would carry that back to Trebizon!

Eleanor enjoyed the party as much as anyone and they all spoiled her and made a fuss of her. Her head was bandaged but it would soon heal up now the stitches were in. Fiona Freeman had a wonderful time, too. She'd long since been finding the real present more fun than the imaginary future! She liked being at Trebizon.

Mrs Mason asked Robbie to drive her back to the bungalow. 'Then you can come back. You young people can enjoy yourselves.' But before she left she invited Tish and Sue to come and have lunch the next day.

While Robbie was away, Rebecca stood on the veranda with Joss and they looked out across the silent playing fields to the distant pine woods that looked purple and mysterious in the dusk.

'It's good to be home,' said Joss.

Then Rebecca told her that she'd been accepted for the Prudential.

Joss was very impressed.

Suddenly Rebecca could be almost light-hearted about it.

'You know, Joss, you really depressed me when you told me I'd look pretty hopeless in the States. But now I've decided I don't care. I mean, I've got to start somewhere!'

Joss stared at Rebecca in dismay.

'I *wondered* if you might have taken that the wrong way.'

'The wrong way?' said Rebecca.

'Well, yes. I wasn't talking about *you* particularly. I meant anyone.' She stared into the distance and said, almost inaudibly: 'Really, I was talking about myself mostly. I'm so fed up with myself! I'm getting worse at tennis, not better.'

Rebecca looked at her in surprise. She suddenly understood.

But she wasn't going to probe. She still wanted to play that match against Joss! More than ever, in fact.

She was just glad that Joss hadn't changed, after all.

'Robbie's back!' she exclaimed, as a familiar figure in jeans appeared from around the corner, where he'd just parked the car.

He came up the steps on to the veranda and put an arm round each girl.

'Any food left in there?' he asked, nodding his

head. Then suddenly, he gave a low whistle.

'Rebeck, I think you must have grown. Here, stand back to back, you two.'

They laughed and did as they were asked.

'I'm right!' said Robbie.

He was.

Rebecca had shot up again since Christmas. She was as tall as Joss now.

Fourth Year Triumph's at

# TREBIZON

Read about
Margot's
triumphs at
**TREBIZON**
in this special
extract...

# <u>ONE</u>
## Back to School

'Nearly back!' thought Rebecca Mason as the taxi took her along the top road that overlooked Trebizon Bay. She gazed across the palely glinting sea to the little island that lay just offshore. It was green and newly washed-looking after a heavy April shower. 'Mulberry Island!' she thought idly, then smiled to herself. 'I'd love to row across there and explore the ruined cottage. We always say we'll do that in the summer term. I wonder if we will?'

She snuggled back comfortably as the cab approached the imposing wrought-iron gates of Trebizon School and slowed down to turn in.

'I wonder what's going to happen this term?'

Some very dramatic things were going to happen. They would never have happened if Sue Murdoch hadn't been introduced to Justin Thomas in the Easter holidays. Rebecca had been there when they met (because it was Robbie Anderson who had introduced them) but since then had never given it a second thought and had no inkling of what it was all going to lead to.

She was just wondering about the coming term in a very general way. And now, as the taxi crawled slowly through the acres of parkland in which the school was set and the main building – once an eighteenth-century manor house – came in sight, she became reflective.

One thing that was *definitely* going to happen was that her parents were coming to the school to meet the Principal, though admittedly that wouldn't be until the end of term. They would be travelling along this very drive and gazing at that beautiful building in the distance, just as she was doing now. Coming down to stay, so they could talk about her future, with Miss Welbeck! Their most recent letter, written as usual on airmail paper, was in Rebecca's luggage somewhere.

*We've been summonsed!* it said. *Miss Welbeck wants to see us at the end of the summer term, as soon as we get back from Saudi for our annual leave. She thinks it's high time we met her and had a proper talk about your future prospects, Becky. After all, we're only home once a year – and she says you'll be taking your mocks next January.*

Apart from the mention of 'mocks', which sent a very slight tremor down Rebecca's spine, quickly banished, the prospect seemed quite pleasurable. It would be nice to have Mum and Dad come to the school for 'consultations'. That phrase 'future prospects' seemed to hold faint promise, somehow. Better make sure she did some work this term. Mustn't let tennis take over her life completely, even though everything to do with tennis seemed to be getting better and better at the moment ... It was all rather heady and exciting, the tennis.

Her friends thought so, too! As the taxi arrived at Court House three of them rushed out to meet her –

'Congratulations, Rebecca!' exclaimed Sally Elphinstone.

'You got as far as the quarter-finals then?' said Margot Lawrence. 'Tish told us the news. Didn't you do well?'

'Clever Rebecca!' Mara Leonodis clapped her hands and laughed, brown eyes glowing. 'You did *so* well at Edgbaston and now you will be selected to go to Eastbourne in August, just you wait and see. Rebecca! You have four tennis rackets now – *four*. And they are all new!'

'I got them free!' laughed Rebecca. 'Here, can you lot help me carry all this stuff? I got them free as long as I don't play with any other make when I go to tournaments. That's easy because they're my favourite racket anyway!'

'I bet you and Joss Vining will be picked as first pair for the school tennis team this term,' said Elf enthusiastically. 'Two Fourth Years being the school's top tennis players, think of it!'

'And then you will go to Eastbourne,' repeated Mara rapturously. 'I shall ask Father to have me flown back to England in August to watch you! You and Joss together, both at Eastbourne.'

The British Junior Grasscourt Championships!

Rebecca laughed and shook her head so vigorously that her fair hair flew in front of her eyes.

'Hang *on*, Mara! Joss will be there I'm sure, but don't count on me making it. My ranking's not high enough – not at the moment, anyway.'

She paid the taxi driver and as the vehicle scrunched away over the gravelled forecourt, the four girls started to sort through the pile of luggage and share it out between them. Changing the subject, Rebecca said:

'Hey, how about Tish, then, scoring all those goals in Holland?'

Although she hadn't seen any sign of them yet, Tish Anderson and Sue Murdoch were Rebecca's two closest friends at Trebizon.

'She's taken some great photos –' began Margot. 'Rebeck!'

With a loud yell of delight a tracksuited figure with short dark curly hair came bounding across the grass, grinning at her.

'Tish!' said Rebecca, with pleasure.

'I was out jogging when I saw your taxi go past!'

'Good. You're just in time to help me get all my stuff upstairs.'

All chattering at once, jostling together, loaded up with Rebecca's luggage, they made for the big front entrance porch of Court House.

Suddenly there was a squeal of brakes behind them and a very luxurious-looking maroon saloon car drew up. A uniformed chauffeur got out and came round to open the rear passenger door.